For Sister Veronica —

The Amethyst
Bottle

Book 3

Linda Shields Allison

*Enjoy Otto's
Journey —*

*Linda Shields Allison
4.5.21*

Published by BookLocker.com, Inc., St. Petersburg, Florida.

Printed on acid-free paper.

The characters and events in this book are fictitious. Any similarity to real persons, living or dead, is coincidental and not intended by the author.

BookLocker.com, Inc.
2020

First Edition

Library of Congress Cataloging in Publication Data
Allison, Linda Shields
The Amethyst Bottle by Linda Shields Allison
Library of Congress Control Number: 2020908006

For My Husband Russell

The Appetizer and
Dessert of My Life

A special thanks to ~

Kate McManus Barkett and Illean Graves
Trautwein for their help and support editing the book.

My brother Robert, who loved the manuscript
and encouraged me not to leave Otto
stranded on the prairie.

My family for always believing in me. You are the
infinite joy in my life that makes me most proud.

Russell Mars for encouraging me to finish the third
book in the journey of the bottle trilogy.

Books by Linda Shields Allison:

The Emerald Bottle

The Bronze Bottle

The Amethyst Bottle

The Characters ~

Otto Stanoff: The Jewish boy from Russia is cruelly taken from his mother when he is ten to work on a Russian cargo ship. He cherishes his mother's beautiful crest with an amethyst stone as a link to his family. He finds life very hard. At thirteen, he escapes when the ship docks in New York. He makes his way living on the streets of Five Points. While there, he comes in possession of a mysterious bottle. When he is offered a job as a wrangler for a wagon train, Otto finds adventure and mishap while crossing the country to California. Along the way, an Indian scout and a young girl help him learn about life.

Cornelius P. McAuliffe: As a favor to a friend, the veteran wagon master takes a chance and hires Otto to work as a wrangler on his wagon train. The captain finds the Russian boy eager to learn and takes him under his wing as he guides a group of emigrants across the prairie and over two mountain ranges into California.

Gray Eagle: While on a vision quest, the young brave becomes injured and Captain Mac saves him from certain death. He takes the Indian on as a scout, and because he can't speak the Lakota language of the Sioux, he calls him Ghost Walker. When Gray Eagle learns that his village has been destroyed and his beloved Little Feather is gone, his life is without meaning. It is a young Russian boy who gives him reason to find life after tragedy.

Little Feather: When the Crow Indians destroy her village, the young girl is captured and taken to live with the Crow tribe.

Victoria Dickerson: The sickly young girl travels west with her family. She spends her days daydreaming and reading books until she meets Otto. The young wrangler asks her to teach him to read and they soon become friends. Through Otto, Victoria learns that life can be an adventure outside of books.

Chandler Dickerson: The lively younger brother of Victoria becomes Otto's friend.

Kirby and Biscuit: The trusted wrangler and cook help Captain McAuliffe guide the emigrants west.

Ivan Stanoff: Otto learns that his older brother is working as a prospector mining gold in California. Otto hopes to find his long lost brother so they might bring their family over from Russia.

Ruby May: The owner of the Ruby Slipper Palace has made a name for herself as a savvy business woman in San Francisco. A long-time friend of Captain McAuliffe, Ruby uses her connections to try to put Otto on track to find his brother.

The Amethyst Bottle

Linda Shields Allison

Preface

When the American Revolutionary War ended in 1781, a steady flow of people clamored west across the United States into vast and uncharted areas of wilderness. Mountain Men came first to trap beaver and hunt deer. Settlers soon followed to farm the valleys and alluvial plains. The land, rich in natural resources, was home to a host of different tribes of Native American Indians. Each tribe lived in harmony with the deer, bison, and bear that Mother Earth provided for them; but their way of life was soon to change forever.

In 1848 a nugget of gold was found at Sutter's Mill in California and the westward migration exploded. Never before in the history of mankind would any territory become so quickly populated with settlers. In just over one hundred years, thousands of pioneers crossed the continent on horseback, in wagons, and on foot. They settled in the mountains and the deserts, on the prairies, and in the lush valleys of the west coast. They pressed onward until American soil stretched from *sea to shining sea.* These hearty men, women, and children tamed the wilderness and made it flourish. By 1869, the Transcontinental Railroad linked the east coast to the west, which helped transport people and goods across the land in five days – and the economy boomed. After the Oklahoma Land Rush of 1889 the United States Census Director was eager to proclaim, "There can hardly be said to be a frontier line."

Although an unprecedented era of American history was ending, the pioneer spirit continued to take shape in the hopes and hardships of immigrants streaming into America from every corner of the globe who dreamed of a better life. The courage of these early settlers helped define a nation of people who embraced the idea of *the land of the free, and the home of the brave.*

Prologue ~ March 1854 - New York City

Otto Stanoff pressed against the wall of Thomas Simpson's medical office so the doctor could measure his height. The thirteen-year-old Russian boy had celebrated a birthday and grown an inch in the month he had been living with the Simpson family. Dr. Simpson had invited Otto to stay with his family in New York after some runaway slaves named, Esther and Bucky, had taken a group of orphans to their new school in Canada. The former slaves, who worked as conductors on the Underground Railroad, were friends of the doctor.

Together they had rescued Otto and some other homeless children from the slums of a pitiless section of Manhattan known as Five Points. The younger children had gone by train to the school with Esther and Bucky, but Otto stayed behind. He had a yearning to go out west.

As luck would have it, Bucky and Doc Simpson told Otto about a friend of his who was a wagon master. He was in Manhattan buying supplies for the men who helped him guide pioneers along the Oregon/California Trail to San Francisco. Bucky had made arrangements for Otto to meet the experienced trail driver, Cornelius P. McAuliffe.

Since gold had been discovered in 1848, scores of pioneers were itching to grab hold of a new life out west. Mac, as he was known to his friends, had questioned Otto and agreed to take the scrappy Russian Jew on as a wrangler to look after the many horses used by him and his men. Cornelius instantly liked the young boy's tenacity, and he made arrangements for Otto to go with him by train, then catch a boat, and finally go by wagon to

Missouri in three weeks. For Otto, the time had flown by with a flurry of activity.

"Why, I've never seen anything quite like it Otto," Doc Simpson declared when he measured Otto against the wall of his infirmary for the third time. "It's true, you've had the appetite of wild boar these past weeks, but I've never seen *anyone* grow as fast as you. An inch in four weeks just has to be a medical wonder," said the doc as he scratched his head.

"Must be the Simpson ladies' good cooking, Doc!" Otto walked over to a chair and carefully placed a loaf of Irish Brown Bread Granny Simpson had made for him on top of his new clothes and alongside a copy of the Bible – a gift from Mrs. Simpson. Otto looked down at the new canvas satchel that would carry all his worldly processions out west.

Dr. Simpson laughed. "Then the women's good cooking must also be brain food, 'cause you've learned the basic fundamentals of reading faster than seems humanly possible! Maybe I should have the Simpson women donate their fine meals to universities to be studied," he chortled. "No, Otto, somehow I don't think it's just the food."

"Ain't that the truth, Doc."

"You mean, "Isn't that the truth, Otto."

"Heck, between your good wife and mother feeding me such fine food, they've barely given me a minute to do anything else, but learn to read and write."

In actual truth, Otto had been a willing pupil in the women's quest to season his education. It seemed his brain was hungry for knowledge. At the end of the first week, he had learned the alphabet, and had finished reading all the pre-primer books owned by the Simpson children. During his second week, he had read every fairy tale in the children's library. Now he was reading passages from the Old Testament in the Bible. The ladies would take turns and read a section to him, then listen as he would tackle the passage aloud. At night, Otto would go over each page until he knew every word and its meaning.

"I think I should write to England to see if there's a name for this type of extreme brain development," Thomas declared with a wink. "If you want to know the truth, Otto, I knew you were smart the first night I met you going through a rubbish-bin in Five Points." Simpson looked fondly at Otto, "We've enjoyed having you in our home. I wish you could stay with our family, but we know you're anxious to find your brother."

"I will miss you, Doc."

Dr. Simpson heard his wife call his name. "Well, Otto, I'll let you finish packing. I have another small gift for you in the other room."

Otto looked down at his new boots and humbly said, "Thanks Doc, but you give Otto so much already."

Dr. Simpson only nodded his head and smiled as he left the room.

Otto reached for the unusual purple bottle resting inside a leather pouch that hung across his shoulder and sighed. It was true. In between eating, he had been studying like a maniac while living with the doctor and his family. However, Otto felt there was something more going on inside him. Ever since he had been given the mysterious bottle by Esther, Otto felt different – stronger both inside and out. He *knew* it must have something to do with the Amethyst Bottle. Yet, it was confusing. Otto could not explain how the curious bottle began to change from the stunning shades of bronze, gold and copper the minute Esther had placed it in his hands. To his amazement, streaks of violet had raced across the bottle until the colors settled into all the varying shade of purple and gold displayed before him now.

Before Esther left, the former slave told him all she knew about the incredible history of the bottle, and how she had gotten it from an Irish girl, named Tara, when according to Esther, the bottle had been emerald green.

Otto thought about the words Esther had said to him just before leaving for Canada. "I understand what you must be feeling, because I was mighty baffled when it happened to me. Just cherish and guard the bottle, Otto, and it may help you find what you're looking for." Then Otto noticed that Esther had turned to where Bucky was playing with the children and whispered, "I know it helped me."

Otto reached inside and pulled the bottle from its neat leather case. The varying tones of violet reminded him of his mother, Natasha, and her beautiful purple enamel crest encrusted with a lovely amethyst stone. The pendant, which hung around Otto's neck from a strip of leather, was shaped in the form of a knight's shield. On the enamel, cast in raised gold, was a two-headed eagle with a crown floating above the heads. A large amethyst stone had been skillfully set into the center of the crown. Otto knew that the crest had been given to his mother by a daughter of Czar Nicholas I. The cousins had loved each other from childhood. The cousin had pressed it into her hand just before Natasha had been banished from the Romanov family for marrying Otto's Jewish father. He also knew that Natasha Stanoff treasured it.

Otto, shivered as he recalled the day he lost both his childhood and his family. The ten-year-old boy had been playing with his sisters' Sophie, Anna, and his baby brother Levi, as their mother, Natasha, hung sheets on the clothesline. Five soldiers raced into the front yard on panting horses with steam spewing from their nostrils. Otto watched in horror, as the horses trampled through his mama's precious garden. They thrust a paper into Natasha's hand and declared that Otto Stanoff was being taken to work on a Russian cargo ship and she had ten minutes to pack his things. Natasha frantically pulled her young son into the house to place some clothes in a bag.

Otto was in a state of panic and asked where he was going.

"You are on the list, my son."

"What list, Mama?"

"The same list that took your brother Ivan from me," she exclaimed.

Large tears streamed from Otto's eyes and he cried, "Please, don't make me go with them, Mama!"

"The czar's soldiers have come and there is nothing we can do," she sobbed. "Listen, Otto, there is so little time."

Otto shook with fear as his mother removed her beloved crest from around her neck. With tears in her eyes, she placed the crest around his neck and carefully tucked it under his sweater. "Guard my necklace well, Otto, and a part of me will always be with you, my son." Otto knew that the crest had been given to his mother by one of her cousins. Mother was a Romanoff and had been raised in a life of privilege. That was before she fell in love with Papa and had been disowned by her family. Once, a gold chain held the beautiful crest, but that had been sold many years before to pay for food and rent. Mama had replaced the gold chain with a sturdy leather strip, and she always wore the crest under her clothing, away from the prying eyes of the villagers who might ask questions about it, or report her to the authorities. She instructed Otto to do the same. Otto hugged his mother one last time. He could smell the homemade lilac soap on her neck and feel the pounding of her heart against his small chest.

The crest was Otto's only link to his family, and he never looked at it in the presence of others for fear it would be taken from him. Instinctively, he reached for the medallion and felt its outline under his new shirt. Otto thought, *And now, incredibly, I have the beautiful Amethyst Bottle.* Otto believed that the mysterious bottle was certain to help him find his brother, Ivan. It was too much of a coincidence. *I'm heading out west with a real job as a wrangler on a wagon train. When Mama gets the letter Dr. Simpson helped me send to Russia, telling her that I am on my way to California to find Ivan, she will be so very proud of me.*

Otto remembered the day that soldiers came to his village in Russia and took his older brother Ivan to work on the roads to make the passage into Poland easier. Ivan wrote home when he could. His sad letters described the poor working conditions and miserable food. Then, one day a letter came all the way from Italy. Ivan had fled Russia and miraculously made his way to a seaport on the eastern shore of that country. There, he signed on with an Italian sailing ship that was taking a shipment of wine and olive oil to New York. The next letter came from that city. Ivan wrote that gold had recently been discovered in California and that he had decided to head out west to seek his fortune. That was the last time Otto had heard from him, because that year, he too had been conscripted by the government to work on a ship. It had been two years since Otto had been in contact with his family, but all that was about to change.

"Write to us, Otto. We'll want to know how you're faring." Dr. Simpson said as he entered the room. A slow grin spread across his face. Thomas pulled a leather-bound journal from behind his back and handed it to Otto. The boy was stunned to see the name **Otto Stanoff** burnt into the leather in fancy lettering.

The doctor coughed. "I bought the journal and burned your name into the leather with a special tool. You'll be seeing a lot of interesting sights, Otto, and I thought it might be a good idea to make a log of your journey. I took the liberty of putting our address here at the back of the book."

Otto felt tears welling in his eyes as he ran his fingers over his name. The wall of distrust that had lived inside him for two years was slowly crumbling. Through the support and love from the Simpson family, Otto had begun to rebuild his faith in human kindness. "I will, Doc. It is special gift. I will use it to record what I see." Carefully, he placed the journal on top of the Bible.

Otto looked at Dr. Simpson. "You have been much kind to me Doc," murmured Otto as he buried his face in the doctor's chest. "I can never pay back all you and your family has given me – the books, the new clothes, and. . .well. . .so much more. I desire to say thanks, and hope I can locate right words in my brain. Part of me would wish to stay here, where I feel safe, but I have a powerful longing to make journey west and find my brother. I see this journey as most important to bring my family back together again."

Thomas Simpson beamed with affection. "I identify with your desire, Otto, and, just for the record, you're going to have no trouble making yourself understood out west."

Simpson looked at his pocket watch and said, "Well, I guess we'd better get you to the train station. We wouldn't want to start you off on the wrong foot with Captain McAuliffe by arriving late for your first day on the job."

"What does this mean – wrong foot?" asked Otto as they walked out the door.

Chapter 1 ~ April 1854 - Elm Grove, Missouri

Otto Stanoff sat on the stump of a tree and sniffed into the breeze. Through a haze of dust that seemed to loiter everywhere in Elm Grove, Otto could smell spring in the air. The spring rains were late in coming, and Otto knew that rainfall was vital to supply the prairie grass for the many horses, mules, and oxen that would carry Otto and about sixty other folks two thousand miles across the wilderness to the gold fields of California. Some of the pioneers planned to pan for gold, but others would make their living by farming. Others planned to open businesses as merchants to cater to the growing towns.

When Otto had arrived at Elm Grove three days ago, he had chuckled at the name of the place just outside of Independence, Missouri. From Otto's viewpoint on the stump, he could only see one or two trees. They didn't look like elm trees, and they definitely were not like any grove he had ever seen as a young boy in Russia. Otto shifted in his seat and looked over his right shoulder. Ramshackle buildings and tents formed a makeshift city that housed the hundreds of people waiting to head west to California, Oregon, or Salt Lake City. The dwellings tilted at odd angles and reminded him of some of the rickety houses he had known when he lived in the slums of Five Points in Manhattan. Although he had been away from that horrible place for only a month, the memory of the year he had spent there trying to stay alive made him shiver with dread. As horrible as it was in Five Points, Otto knew it was better than the years he had spent being forced to work on a Russian cargo ship. He also knew he had been smart to jump ship in New York and try and make it on his own, as his brother Ivan had done. Otto washed the thoughts from his mind. Carefully, he closed his new journal, and stored his pencil in the pocket of his new flannel shirt.

Otto soaked up the warm afternoon sun and smiled at the scene before him. He watched toddlers playing at their mothers' heels as the women washed clothes or peeled potatoes for dinner. The children made him homesick for his own brothers and sisters, and the mother he had been so cruelly taken from in Russia when he was only ten. He gazed at the men, huddled in groups, arguing over what animals were best for pulling wagons across the prairie – or how much salt, coffee, and flour would be needed for the six-month journey, and Otto wished his father was still alive.

His heart began to quicken. In the distance he saw the wagon master motion for Otto to join him where he stood near the horses. Cornelius P. McAuliffe was not a mean man, but he was a natural born leader and a bit gruff around the edges, as leaders sometimes are. The tall lean man with russet-brown eyes and a ruggedly handsome face commanded the respect of others, and usually got it with his quiet no-nonsense manner. Born the third son of a southern aristocratic plantation owner, Mac knew that he would never inherit his father's land and that suited him just fine. He had always had a peculiar feeling about his father owning the slaves who worked on his plantation. To him, it just seemed wrong. Besides which, he never liked to stay in one place too long. McAuliffe had been a wagon master for eight years. At forty-five, he had never married and the wandering life of a trail master suited his lifestyle. Otto admired his rugged good looks, and was grateful that McAuliffe had hired him on as a wrangler. Otto desperately wanted to please his new boss more than anything.

Otto leapt off the tree stump and brushed the dust off his new pants. "I'm coming, sir!" he shouted.

Otto ran over to Captain McAuliffe and waited as the trail master gave instructions to a cowboy named Kirby. The man had been on many trail drives, and the captain trusted that Kirby would do whatever he asked to get the job done.

McAuliffe flipped to a page in his ledger and said, "Check on the Dickerson family next. Inventory a list of the supplies they've laid in and make certain they have the right amount of provisions for the trip. Look over their oxen to see if they're fit enough for the long trek west. Oh, and Kirby, mention that I'll stop by later to answer any questions they might have. Tell, them to have two hundred dollars ready as my fee, and that I'll collect the remaining two hundred when I've safely delivered them to California. Check back with me before you move on to the next wagon. I think we'll inventory Isaac Wise and his family."

"Sure thing, boss," declared Kirby. He tipped his hat to McAuliffe and headed in the direction of the Dickerson's wagon.

Otto had met the Dickerson family on his first day in Elm Grove. Tony and Julia had invited him to share lunch with them and meet their children. Chandler, a hearty sandy-haired boy was two-years younger that Otto. He was full of life and had an impish gleam in his intelligent blue eyes. Otto knew that they would get along fine. The Dickerson's daughter, Victoria, was thirteen – same as Otto. He thought the girl seemed pale in color and a bit shy. She had thick reddish-blond hair and a smattering of freckles that dotted her nose. Otto could not tell what color her eyes were because Victoria spent most of the afternoon with her nose buried in a book. Otto was already wondering how he might persuade her to let him have a crack at reading it when she was finished.

The Dickerson farm had been sold in Springfield, Illinois and they were heading to California to join Julia's brother and his family who owned a farm in the Sacramento Valley. It was a risk to sell everything and move, but after watching Victoria struggle with a series of illnesses that had left the girl bedridden the last few winters, Julia thought the milder climate in California might improve their daughter's health. Two toddlers, Jessica and Christina, completed the members of the family.

McAuliffe turned his attention to Otto. He stamped the butt of his cigarette into the dirt and immediately began to roll another one from a cloth bag filled with tobacco and a tiny square of white paper. "How are you getting on Otto? Is everyone treating you okay?"

Otto glanced over at Bull. The burly cowboy was repairing a section of fence that held a dozen horses penned inside a makeshift corral. "Sure, Captain McAuliffe, everyone treating Otto okay," he lied.

In actuality, Bull had made Otto's life uncomfortable over the past two days. Otto thought that maybe it was some kind of prank that cowboys inflicted on all newly hired hands. Being a cabin boy on a Russian ship, Otto knew first hand about being the object of some of the sailor's jokes and torments. He was used to it, but still he found it annoying to wake up on his second morning in Elm Grove to discover that water had been poured into the brand new boots Dr. Simpson had given him. Otto knew it hadn't rained over night. Then Otto noticed Bull snickering at him as he poured the water out of his boot. Otto knew that the wet ankle boots would give him blisters, so he decided to go barefoot that morning and give the shoes time to dry out. This was really no hardship for him. His feet had grown calloused from going without shoes living in the slums of Five

Points after being beaten by a pair of thugs who stole his only shoes.

When Otto went to check on the boots that afternoon, he noticed that sand had been poured into the boots clear up to the top. He tried to dump it out, but a fair amount remained stuck against the sides of the wet interior of the boots. Otto knew to outwit his tormentor, he would have to use his brain. So, he took the shoes over to the Dickerson's wagon and found Julia kneading bread dough. He told her that he had been the victim of an unfortunate mishap by the creek and wondered if he could please dry his boots on the seat of their covered wagon. Julie said she would be only too happy to oblige.

Funny thing though, the next morning when Otto went to get the boots, they were not only dry, but cleaned of all traces of sand and had been shined with polish, as well. He went over where Mrs. Dickerson was making biscuits for breakfast to say thanks, but she had only shrugged her shoulders and said, "Oh my, Otto, I plum forgot they were there. I'm glad you remembered where you put them." She then invited him to stay for breakfast, but he told her he had already eaten and was needed by the trail master.

McAuliffe expertly rolled his cigarette and licked the end of the paper with his tongue. The captain lit it with a match and turned his attention to his new wrangler. "Are you getting enough to eat?"

"Yes, sir, cook's food is good."

"There's nothing fancy about Biscuit's cooking, but there'll be plenty of it. Every once in a while he'll make a pie from some wild berries or apples, and that'll bring the boys running to his dinner bell."

Otto made a mental note to ask Mrs. Dickerson what a pie was.

"Tell me, Otto, what do you remember about what I showed you yesterday?"

Otto cleared his throat. "You told me that horses are smart and useful animals but need to be groomed by people so they won't get sick. You showed me how the body, tail, and mane must be brushed everyday. I should check horses for cuts when I'm brushing and clean cuts with liniment so horses won't get sick. Then you showed me how to check the hooves for stones with the hoof pick and to tell you if there is any swelling in horses' legs." Otto wrinkled his brow and said, "Oh, and I should check saddles and blankets for stickers and burrs each night, 'cause that could cause horses...let me think...a darn sight of misery."

The trail driver laughed. The boy had repeated his lesson almost word for word. "That's good, Otto. For a boy that's only been in America for a year, you speak English better than a lot of emigrants I've taken west"

"In Five Points it was learn English or starve," said Otto.

Mac laughed again. Then a hacking cough erupted from his lungs. The wagon master frowned as he looked at the smoke rising from his cigarette. "Smoking is a filthy habit, Otto. Do yourself a favor and never take it up."

"Yes, sir."

McAuliffe liked the Russian boy and had a feeling that Otto was going to make a good wrangler. Driving a group of greenhorn easterners west was hard work. Most folks had never been more than twenty miles from their homes. He needed a good wrangler to take care of the horses his men rode. It was important to rotate the horses each day, and give them a rest. A two-thousand mile trek across the wilderness could wear a horse out. Mac had a good feeling about the newly hired hand and thought he would make a fine addition to the two cowboys, an

Indian scout, and one victuals and provisions' wagon cook already in his employment.

"You've not only grown like a fungus since we first met in New York, Otto, but you seem to have the right bits and pieces to make a good wrangler. Not only that, you're smart. You take to learning like a fish to a worm. Now you gotta realize, Otto, it's not enough to know how to care for a horse. To understand horses in general you must also learn to become a good rider."

Otto opened his eyes wide in disbelief. It had taken Otto a few days to understand the unusual southern drawl of the trail master. His manner of speaking was different from Dr. Simpson – as though the vowel sounds were drawn out like a sleepy yawn. Although he did not always understand *every* word, Otto generally got the idea of what was expected of him thanks to McAuliffe's slow way of talking. So, when Otto heard Mac's unhurried accent sputter out the words *good rider,* he nearly choked. He knew that he would be responsible for the care and feeding of the horses; he did not know that he was going to be allowed to ride them. Otto's heart pounded in his chest with a mixture of excitement and fear. His mouth went as dry as the dust on his boots, and he could only nod.

"Listen careful-like, Otto. Now, a good rider will get the best out of his horse with the least amount of strain. Horses are smart, and they'll try a man's patience if the rider will let them. A horse needs to know who's in charge. By nature, horses will lash out through fear or anger in three ways. They'll rear up and run off, then again they might bite, or they'll kick you with their back hooves. Always let them know you're in charge. But at the same time you should be gentle but firm, and the horse will serve you well. Are you ready to learn how to ride?"

Otto was too scared to speak and all he could do was nod.

Sensing the boy's fear, McAuliffe bent down so he was eye level and lowered his voice, "Look, Otto, a horse can smell fear in a man, so you best shake off those feelings with a couple of deep breaths."

Otto swallowed a gulp of air.

McAuliffe laughed. "You're gonna be just fine. Now go over there. My Indian scout is waiting to show you how to saddle-up. There's no one on this wagon train that's a better rider than Ghost Walker. Listen to him and you'll become a good rider too.

Chapter 2 ~ April 1854 - Elm Grove, Missouri

Over the past three days, Otto had seen the Indian around camp. In truth, he continually found himself staring at the scout they called Ghost Walker. Otto had never seen a real Indian. In Five Points, there was a drunk who hung around the bars begging for money. He was supposed to be from a tribe of Indians called the Iroquois, but that cheerless man in dirty clothes looked nothing like the imposing figure that Otto was walking toward.

This Indian was tall with shiny black hair parted down the middle and worn long like a horse's tail. A thin strip of rawhide tied the hair at the back of the head. Several blue and white beads had been fastened to the ends of the rawhide. A small single white feather had been cleverly tied to the rawhide and hung loosely facing downward against the back of the hair. His face was handsomely set off with high cheek bones and piercing black eyes. The Indian scout had skin the same warm golden-brown color of the teakwood that Otto had polished as a cabin boy on the Russian ship. Otto noticed that Ghost Walker also wore a beautifully polished arrowhead fastened with rawhide around his neck. He had observed the Indian stroking the superbly crafted stone with his right hand when he thought no one was looking at him. For some reason, the arrowhead reminded Otto of his mother's crest that was so dear to his heart, and Otto wondered if the stone had a special meaning for the scout.

Each morning, Otto had seen the Indian bathing down by the stream in his loin cloth. He was lean with not an ounce of fat on his body – yet his arms and legs were muscular and strong.

Otto felt like a small insignificant beetle compared to this perfect specimen of health. Otto noticed that Ghost Walker did not dress in the clothes of the white man. He wore buckskin pants and a matching shirt made of pale soft leather. Instead of boots, the Indian wore leather moccasins on his feet, and he moved gracefully in them like a tiger Otto had once seen prowling near his village in Russia. Otto wondered how old the Indian was. It was baffling, but he thought that Ghost Walker looked both young and old at the same time. It was almost as though the Indian had the body of a young man but the spirit of an old man. Otto felt certain that he and the Indian could have a lot in common, and he desperately wanted to get to know him better.

Only yesterday, Otto had tried to draw the quiet young scout into conversation by asking him where McAuliffe stored the extra brushes for the horses. But the Indian had only pointed to three brushes resting in clear sight on an old wooden table, and Otto had felt foolish and small.

Otto let out a long slow breath of air as he walked up to where the Indian stood whispering softly into his horse's ear. "Good morning, Ghost Walker. I am Otto." Otto groaned inwardly at the silly sound of his words.

Ghost Walker moved his head a few inches away from his pony to look at Otto, but the frisky mare wanted the Indian's attention, and she nuzzled him with her nose and flipped her white tail in the air. Otto smiled thinking the horse acted just like a child who wanted the full attention of its mother.

The animal was the most unusual horse Otto had ever seen. The mare was reddish-brown with large white spotted markings on her body. In contrast, the horse's face was completely reddish-brown with the exception of one strange mark on the forehead in the same white color of the tail. Otto thought that the mark reminded him of something, but he couldn't quite piece it out in his mind. Ghost Walker whispered something to the mare in his native tongue then turned to the boy. Otto noticed that the horse obeyed the Indian by standing completely still. Otto had never seen anything quite like it.

"Trail Boss say me teach boy to ride horse. You ever ride horse?"

Otto gulped, "No...sir."

"Before boy ride, first must know how to put saddle on horse."

Otto spent the better part of an hour putting on and taking off the blanket and saddle – cinching straps and attaching the bridle and bit to the head. It was only when he had done it for the fifth time that Ghost Walker was satisfied that the horse was properly fitted and that Otto was ready for his first lesson. Ghost Walker had chosen a small and gentle brown mare for Otto to ride. From where Otto stood, the horse seemed as tall as the mast on a ship.

"Rider must always mount horse from here." The Indian pointed to the left side of the horse. "Put foot in stirrup and pull up with hands on saddle horn." Ghost Walker pointed to Otto's left foot and a leather-handle sticking up from the front part of the saddle.

Otto noticed that the cowboy, named Bull, had finished the repair on the fence and was scratching the heavy crop of whiskers on his chin. The amused cowboy was chuckling under his breath from where he sat watching on the top rail of the corral. Otto looked up at the horse and prayed that he could even get his hands on the saddle horn – it seemed so high up, but he was determined not to fail in front of the oafish cowboy. The Russian boy adjusted the leather case at his side which encased the bottle. Gritting his teeth and rubbing his two hands together, he carefully placed his foot in the stirrup. He wrapped the tips of his fingers around the saddle horn and grunted aloud as he pulled the weight of his body up into the saddle. For an instant, Otto thought he was going to topple over the other side of the horse and fall to the ground. But thankfully, the horse only took a few steps forward and then stopped, and Otto was able to steady himself in the saddle. Ghost Walker adjusted the stirrups to the length of Otto legs.

"Yer lookin' like a real cowboy, now," teased Bull. "Maybe ya can learn to ride Injun style like yer red-skinned teacher,"

Otto looked at the Indian and thought his skin looked nothing like the color red. He wondered if Ghost Walker was annoyed, but the scout did not seem to be bothered by Bull's taunting comments. In fact, he never even looked over in the direction of where the massive cowboy sat.

Otto watched Ghost Walker mount his horse. The Indian did not have a saddle on the brown and white pinto, and he seemed to spring off the ground with his left foot as his right leg swept over the back of his pony in one fluid motion. Otto was in awe of the effortless way the brave ascended the back of his horse.

The motion caused Otto's mare to skitter a few paces sideways. The muscles in Otto's thighs tightened against the saddle. He prayed that he would not fall off, and as if in answer, the gentle brown mare settled to a stop. Otto gripped the saddle horn until the knuckles in his hands turned white. His stomach flipped like the rocking motion of a ship as he adjusted his position on the horse. Then he remembered McAuliffe's words. *A horse can smell fear in a man.* Otto drew in several deep breaths with his nose to relax his body. *I can do this, thought Otto. Heck, I've faced storms at sea that would scare the feathers off a chicken.* Otto relaxed his grip on the saddle horn and looked across to where the Indian sat facing him comfortably astride his pony.

All of a sudden, it came to Otto, and he smiled. *The unusual marking on the horse's forehead that I wondered about earlier looks like a small white feather!* He glanced closer at the mare and it became as clear as water to him. The white mark on the Indian's pony looked exactly like a delicately curved feather suspended weightless in air just as if it had been tossed there by the wind.

Ghost Walker interrupted his thoughts by declaring, "Today we walk horse. Rider must have good balance." He guided his horse over to Otto. "Shorten reins...hold here. This movement tells horse to go slow. No...not like that. Bit is too tight. Relax hands. Let fingers move reins in and out with motion of horse's head. Boy must be one with horse."

Otto wished to make an impression on the Indian, so he willed himself to relax as Ghost Walker guided Otto and his horse away from the corral and the snickering sounds of Bull.

Chapter 3 ~ June 1851 - Indian Territory

The young fifteen-year-old brave known as Gray Owl, to his Sioux tribe, had been sent into the wilderness alone. On the verge of manhood, the young boy was on a mission to discover his vision-quest. It was a ritual all Sioux boys went through before entering into manhood. During this time alone, a boy would fast, meditate, and pray to his ancestors until he reached a trance-like state. Gray Owl was told that a dream would come to him. It was believed that this vision would determine and guide him in taking his place as an adult member of the tribe. Gray Owl had been taught from childhood that all his success in life would depend on having a strong vision. It was especially important to Gray Owl because his father was a shaman. The medicine man held a key position as the spiritual and healing advisor for his tribe, and the young warrior hoped to follow in his father's footsteps. He needed a worthy vision to ensure his place as the future shaman for his people, the Sioux.

Gray Owl had been with only a little food and water for two days. He had called his ancestors for guidance but to his dismay, no vision had come to him. The young brave, though weak from hunger and thirst, was determined to stay alone in the wilderness until his great Sioux ancestors came to him with a vision of such magnitude that his family would burst with pride.

From the yellow grass of the prairie, Gray Owl looked up and noticed a bald eagle circling the cloudless sky. Thinking that the graceful bird might be a sign from Mother Earth, he decided to climb up the face of a large out-cropping of rocks to get a better view of the majestic bird. As he scaled up the side of the granite, Gray Owl admired the beautiful wing-span of the eagle and thought of his friend – a young Sioux girl known to his people as Little Feather.

Little Feather was soft and delicate like her name. She possessed lovely brown eyes and a full mouth that always held a happy smile. She had been born two summers after Gray Owl. He and Little Feather had played together as children and Gray Owl had loved her for most of his life.

The young brave knew that she loved him too. *When my vision-quest is completed, I will be strong in body and in spirit,* he thought. *I will take my place in the tribe. I will hunt and kill a hundred bison. I will ride my pony well and take part in many coups of our enemy. Then, my ancestors will help me find the courage to ask Coyote Tail whether Little Feather might become my wife.* With a worthy vision-quest and Little Feather at his side, Gray Owl felt confident that he would secure his place as an important man in his tribe.

Gray Owl was surprised at how much effort it took to climb up the steep face of the rock. The lack of food and water made even simple tasks hard. He had climbed almost to the top of the rock when, from out of nowhere, a large black crow flew straight at his head. Black feathers slapped against the boy's face. Gray Owl loosened his hold on the rock with one hand to drive the bird away. His feet slipped out from under him, but he held firm with one hand which was gripped tightly inside a crevice in the rock.

"Go away pesky crow! Have I disturbed the nest where your babies sleep? If so, I am sorry, but I will not harm your children." Liberated from the attack by the black bird, Gray Owl reached up with his loose hand to better secure himself to the rock. Abruptly, the crow swept in again and began to claw at his head.

The sudden movement unnerved the young Indian, and for a second time caused him to lose his grip on the rock. Feeling already weak and dizzy from lack of food and water, Gray Owl could not hold on. The boy's hand inched away from where it was anchored, and he felt himself slipping.

Gray Owl was angry with the crow. As gravity took hold and the boy began to fall from the rock, he had the odd sensation that he was descending slowly – as in a trance. He reached for the branch of a small tree, absurdly trying to grow out of a crack in the granite. But, he only felt his skin scrape cruelly against the bark as it broke off in his hand, and he slithered thirty feet down the face of the rock. He landed hard – breaking two ribs as he smacked against the yellow grass. Gray Owl lay unconscious for the rest of the day.

When he awoke it was dark. From his position on his back Gray Owl saw thousands of stars in the sky. The night was warm, but the boy shivered from shock – not only from the jolt of the fall, but from a strange and unsettling dream – so real that it filled his mind with terrifying visions. The horrified boy shook when he remembered fierce angry men with faces streaked in brightly-colored paint riding into his village on horseback. Gray Owl realized that his cheeks were drenched in tears. At first, the young brave was ashamed to have been crying in his sleep. Suddenly, he wrenched from a sharp pain in his lungs as he attempted to wipe the tears from his cheeks. The sudden pain pushed the dream from his mind.

Gray Owl remembered the crow flying into his head and his fall from the rock. He thought that he had broken his ribs, but decided that he must try and make his way back to his village to get treated by his father. If he remained wounded on the prairie, he would become easy prey for a mountain lion or a pack of coyotes. The boy tried to sit up. He nearly passed out in pain, but forced himself to his feet. Slowly, he began to stumble across the dry prairie grass toward his village.

The boy walked all night. His lips were swollen from thirst. Try as he might, he could not concentrate on the task of finding his village because the strange dream kept popping into his thoughts. The disturbing images had been so real – so lifelike, and suddenly he gasped as he recalled the worst of it.

In his vision, Gray Owl had seen the enemy of the Sioux, a tribe of Indians called the Crow, riding into his village to kill his people, to steal their horses, to burn his village. He grimaced as he recalled the high-pitched yelps of the painted warriors as they set fire to his parents' tipi as they slept. Gray Owl choked back a scream as he remembered the flames that engulfed his village, and the sight of a lone white feather floating skyward with the rising of thick black smoke.

Chapter 4 ~ June 1851 - Indian Territory

Cornelius P. McAuliffe sat on his horse, Dickens, and surveyed the mid-morning sky over the prairie. He was happy to be away from the wagon train. As wagon master, he sometimes felt like a mother hen to a band of moody children who required his constant help. He settled arguments, waylaid their fears, and offered reassurance over the least little things. When the needs of the emigrants played too heavily on his nerves, McAuliffe would tell his trail hands that he was going on a little hunting expedition to provide fresh meat for the company. The men understood that what the captain really needed was some time alone. From past experience, the trail master found that the smell of fresh venison or bison roasting over hot flames and a day of rest usually put everyone in the group in a better mood – including Mac.

The wagon master had felt fortunate to bring down a lone male deer he found eating the bark off a tree at dawn. After fashioning a travois with some sturdy branches of a tree, McAuliffe began dragging the food back to camp with his horse.

"Whoa, Dickens," Mac whispered to his horse as he pulled on the reins and stopped. The trail master removed his rifle from its cradle and gently rested it across his lap. In the distance, he saw a lone Indian brave walking across the dried prairie grasses. Mac did not want any trouble, so he decided to rest Dickens and let the Indian pass on to wherever he was going. From his seat on the horse, McAuliffe could see that the young brave had no weapons. On closer inspection, he noticed that the Indian seemed to shuffle as he walked. Mac pulled out his bag of tobacco and began to roll himself a cigarette.

As he sat in his saddle smoking in the morning light, Mac watched the brave veer left, which altered his forward march into what ultimately became a circle. The wagon master reached down to carefully snuff out the hot ember from his cigarette butt onto the heel of his boot. The veteran wagon master knew how easy it was to start a prairie fire. When he looked up he could see nothing on the horizon but yellow grass. For one strange second, Mac wondered if he had seen a ghost walking across the prairie.

"Go, boy." Cornelius moved his horse forward in the general direction of where he thought he had last seen the Indian. He carefully scanned the area to see if anything looked suspicious. The last thing he needed was a sneaky Indian brave popping out of the grass to try and steal his deer. With caution, McAuliffe ordered his horse to stop a few yards from where the Indian lay crumpled in the tall prairie grass. He slowly dismounted from his horse and readied his rifle. As McAuliffe closed the space between himself and the Indian, he could see that this boy had had an accident. The young brave was covered in cuts and scratches. The trail driver turned on his heel and swiftly walked back to where his horse stood munching on grass. He untied a worn canteen from his saddle and returned to the injured boy.

McAuliffe lifted the boy's head off the ground and poured a small amount of water into his mouth. The liquid began to revive the Indian almost immediately, and the boy opened and closed his mouth like a fish. "Slow down now, boy – take it slow." Mac was unsure if the Indian understood what he was saying, but the soothing tone of his voice seemed to calm the boy in distress.

At length, Gray Owl opened his eyes. He was too weak to be afraid of the white man leaning over him offering water. All he knew was that someone had come to his aid, and he was very grateful. In the back of his mind, he realized he would have to get well so that he could find his way back to his people.

Mac looked down at the boy and said, "I don't know where you came from, but right now I'm gonna take you back to camp with me. I reckon your people will track you there, and they can take you off my hands. Lord knows, I don't want any trouble, but I can't leave you here to become buzzard food." He lifted the boy into his arms and gently laid him on top of the dead deer. "It's not a feather bed, but you'll be alright, boy," the trail driver said as he tied the boy securely to the travois.

Time is important on a wagon train heading west, and McAuliffe would stop for no one – especially an injured Indian boy. Wagon masters and emigrants alike were well aware of the many articles written about an ill-fated group who came to be known as the Donner Party. Traveling west in 1846, the group split off from the main wagon train to take an uncharted route known as Hastings Cutoff. The company lost valuable time in the Wasatch Mountains. Hauling their wagons over streams and up steep slopes made passage for their group almost impossible.

It was late in the season when they tried to cross the Sierra Nevada Mountain Range. On the second day of November, the Donner Party became trapped as a blinding snowstorm hit their camp below the summit. Twenty-two feet of snow fell all throughout the winter. The continual blizzards made it impossible to travel or to be rescued, and the people began to starve.

That fateful winter would later become known as the worst snowstorm of the century. Newspapers all across the east coast of America reported the grizzly details of the famished people who resorted to eating those unfortunate souls who had died from starvation before them. The incident shocked and disturbed the nation.

That year, McAuliffe had heard rumors about a shortcut called Hastings Cutoff, but he had refused the impulse to venture into the unknown, and the trail master safely led his group through to California traveling along the established trail.

Back at camp, the wagon master was in a quandary as what to do with the injured boy. McAuliffe approached a kindly preacher heading to San Francisco to educate the gold miners on the evils of drinking and gambling, and he offered to help. So while the Indian boy recovered in the back of the preacher's covered wagon, the wagon train rolled west. Mac stopped by each evening to check on the boy's progress.

It took two weeks before the boy's ribs were healed enough to move. Mac taught the boy a few English words and the boy taught Mac a few Sioux words. But mostly, they communicated with points and gestures and pictures. Mac showed the boy a map of his wagon train heading west with the setting sun. The boy roughly sketched the whereabouts of his village while frantically pointing back in the other direction. It took some doing, but McAuliffe was able to show the boy on his map how he would be coming back along the same trail in a few moons and that he would help him find his village on the return trip east. The boy nodded in somber silence.

Over the next few weeks the boy watched and listened and learned. The two, whom fate had brought together, found that they were comfortable in each other's company. Despite their ages, they developed a relationship founded on mutual respect, and the two learned many things from each other. Cornelius did not know the young boy's name, so over time, he began to call him Ghost Walker.

When the boy had been with the wagon train for two months, McAuliffe found it useful to take the Indian with him to hunt for food. He soon became astounded at the way his young Indian friend could track the footprints of wild game. The Indian could pick up the trail of anything – including the traces of other tribes of Indians in the region. He seemed to know how many were in their party and when they had broken camp.

One day, the two friends were tracking a mountain lion that had been terrorizing the horses at night. They had stopped their horses on a ridge and were inspecting some tracks in the dirt. The Indian boy, who could communicate some words in broken English, surprised Mac when he asked, "What means this name you say of me, Ghost Walker?"

The trail master drew in the tobacco of his cigarette and coughed. He had grown very fond of this boy. He hoped he hadn't in some way offended him with the name. "When I saw you that day on the prairie, I wondered if you were real, or some kind of a ghost walking in the distance," offered McAuliffe. "You looked so lost and, in truth, half dead like a spirit…a ghost. Somehow, the name just fit. If you can tell me what your true name is, I'd be more than happy to call you that."

The Indian boy thought of the name given to him by his people, Gray Owl. He knew that it would be easy to make this name understood to McAuliffe. He breathed in deeply and thought of the contented life he had known with his people, the Sioux. He thought of his father and mother. He saw the smiling face of Little Feather – and finally he remembered the vision of death and fire in his village – a vision that still haunted him in his dreams at night. Gray Owl looked across at the tall lean man and said, "Ghost Walker – good name for this Indian."

True to his word, McAuliffe took Ghost Walker back to his village on the return trip east. The scene that lay before the two friends tore into their hearts. As McAuliffe and Ghost Walker surveyed the burnt skeleton of a once productive village, the devastation stood out in stark contrast to the tranquil river and shimmering cottonwood trees in the distance.

"What happened?" McAuliffe asked in horror. "Who would've done this?"

Ghost Walker was too stunned to speak. He slipped off his horse and walked through the rubble that was once his home. In the six months since he had been gone, weeds had grown over and covered the once smooth earth where women skinned buffalo hides for blankets, and young boys played games – where wise men sat around the fire talking of the old days, and young girls danced by the light of the campfire. All that was left of the magnificent tipis were the charred-black remains of lodge poles. Ghost Walker muttered, "This death from our enemy tribe, the Crow."

The young brave ran to the spot where his parent's tipi once stood and fell to his knees. He savagely burrowed his hands into the soil hoping to find something from his former life. When he scrapped his finger on the sharp edge of an arrowhead, he did not feel the pain. He pulled the finely tooled stone from the scorched earth and folded it so tightly in his hand that it continued to cut into his flesh.

The young Indian brave grew into manhood that very moment when he raised the bloodied arrowhead to the sky and screamed out in his native tongue. "You are my enemy, Crow! You have taken everything that was dear to me. You have taken my family. You have taken my girl. You have taken my name. From this day forward, Gray Owl is dead. I know only the one called Ghost Walker."

Chapter 5 ~ May 1854 -Overland Trail

Preevyet (hello).

It is Sunday, our one day of the week to rest, so I'm writing to you again in my new journal. This way, I feel like we are here together, and I can practice writing in new language. We have been on what my boss calls Overland Trail for two weeks now traveling through country so flat, I think I could kick a cabbage, and it would roll along the grass for one hundred miles. Twenty seven wagons, with covers all made from sturdy canvas like sails of a ship, are home to sixty five people heading west under the expert guidance of our wagon master, Cornelius P. McAuliffe. Let me say that he is the nicest man I have ever had the pleasure to work for. He is tough yet very kind, and I like him so much. Our wagons travel in a long line, and I've noticed that, just like when I was a small child in our village at home, the families seemed to settle into smaller groups as they figure out who they like and have something in common with. Now, with all that sorted out, people just are happy to keep their place in line much like our family sitting in the same seats around dinner table.

Leading the train are Captain McAuliffe's two wagons. Our cook sleeps in our food wagon. It is filled with all the supplies and stove for fixing our meals. Two of Mr. McAuliffe's men, Bull and Kirby, bunk (this means sleep) alongside the captain and me in the other wagon. You would never believe, but there is a real live Indian who is a tracker and scout for our train. His name is Ghost Walker, and he is teaching me to ride a horse. He mostly likes to sleep outside under the wagon if the weather is nice. I am very anxious to get to know this Indian, but he does not talk much and seems to be happiest in his own company. I love my job as wrangler. When not caring for the horses, I have much freedom to explore.

I have made friends with a nice family called Dickerson, and they are next in line. I like them very much, especially their boy Chandler. He showed me how to set out traps at night to catch catfish. This funny looking fish, which has the whiskers of a cat, tastes wonderful when cooked over an open flame. Tony and Julia Dickerson have two little girls, and one more child. Their daughter, Victoria, has been harder to get to know. She was sickly last winter and seems to spend most of her time reading. I want to make friends with her so she might help me continue my studies with learning to read in English, but I have not thought of how I might approach her.

A Jewish family from Germany named Wise is next. Isaac and Rachel Wise have three little girls. They are going to San Francisco to open a shoe shop. Mr. Wise told me that there is a big need for cobblers out west. He says that another German man named Levi Strauss is having success making sturdy pants out of canvas for the gold miners, and he is hoping to do the same with his leather shoes and boots. Being under the rules of the wagon train, we cannot observe all the traditions of Sabbath which, as you know, begins on Friday with the setting of the sun and carries through Saturday until nightfall. The family was so kind and invited me to their camp last Friday evening to drink a small sip of wine for kiddush and to share in the blessing of the hallah bread. It was wonderful to say the prayers in Yiddish again by the light of the Sabbath candles. It reminded me so much of Papa that I wanted to cry. I said prayers for you, Mama, and for everyone in our family.

The third passenger in line is a fancy English gentleman by name of Sir Nigel Churchstone who is traveling alone except for his butler – a quite formal man-servant called Simon Walton. When we break for our midday meal, in what the captain refers to as nooning, the butler sets up a stylish little table complete with napkins and a tablecloth. Simon then serves Sir Nigel cheese, biscuits and tea on fancy china. Chandler and I brought Sir Nigel a catfish one day and he was so happy, that he invited us to take tea with him. I felt like I could have been dining with Czar Nicholas himself! This is quite an adventure. If things go as

smoothly in future, getting to California will be
as simple as peeling potatoes.
Do sbedanya (goodbye).

Your faithful son ~ Otto Stanoff (age 13)

Bump…creek…heave…thud…groaned the wagons wheels as they pressed forward behind the mighty oxen. On days when the weather was fine, the wagon train could make twenty miles across the flat dry prairie grass. Twice it had rained hard, and the wagon wheels slogged through mud and wet grass like a tortoise on sand. On those days the wagon master was satisfied with ten. Behind the line of wagons came the *cow column*. Milk cows, spare oxen and horses were driven by men and boys on horseback under the direction of Bull. Captain McAuliffe and Ghost Walker led the train as Kirby rode up and down the line making sure the wagons rolled smoothly and there were no problems. Each night the train pulled into the safety of a circle. The oxen, cattle and horses were set loose to graze as men took turns guarding the whole operation under the prairie stars.

Otto was busiest early in the morning and again just after the sunset flamed in the west. He woke up before dawn to pick out the work horses for the day and to saddle them up for McAuliffe and his men to ride. He would then lead the horses over to the cook wagon where the captain and his men were eating breakfast. Biscuit would hand Otto a plate of bacon, beans, biscuits and coffee as the captain and his men headed for their places in the line.

Each evening, it was Otto's job to gather together the horses that had been ridden by McAuliffe and his men that day. He would unsaddle, brush, and check them over for sores. Otto had offered to brush Ghost Walker's horse, but the Indian seemed to enjoy taking care of his own pony. If one of the horses came up lame or needed rest, Otto would switch that horse out for a fresh one and let the tired horse walk behind with the cow column.

Otto liked his job and the freedom he had during midday to do as he pleased if he wasn't needed by the captain. He and Chandler Dickerson had become fast friends. They enjoyed passing the time walking beside the wagons gathering dried branches and sticks into gunnysacks for Biscuit and Julia Dickerson to use for the cooking fires. Otto talked about his family in Russia and Chandler shared what his life had been like in Illinois.

"The best thing about going west is no school," Chandler remarked. "My teacher, Miss Nettles, enjoyed making my life miserable. She liked the girls best – especially this bossy know-it-all, Mary Ellen Marty. I called her Mary Ellen Smarty Pants. Once she punished me for tying Mary Ellen's hair ribbons to the back of her chair, and I had to stand with my nose to the blackboard for an entire afternoon. It was worth it though to see little *Miss Smarty* pop up to answer a question only to get jerked back into her seat. If that wasn't enough, I had to take a note home to my parents and they made me tie string to the bean poles in the garden since they said I was so fond of tying things. I spent a week in the dirt. It would have been longer if Victoria hadn't helped me."

"In Russia, Jews could not go to school with other children. Only boys were allowed to go to Temple and learn from Rabbi Solomon, and if a boy got in trouble he must shovel snow for Rabbi after school. I never wanted to worry Mama by being a problem. She had much sadness after Papa died and Ivan was taken away."

"Otto, how'd your father die?"

Otto's voice grew soft and Chandler had to strain to listen to the words of his friend. "When I was a young boy of four, Papa was taken one night by soldiers when he was on his way home from working at Temple for Rabbi Solomon. When he does not come home that night, Mama goes to the rabbi in the morning. He tells her that people say that Papa has been taken away by soldiers. Mama, she goes to army prison and asks if Papa is there. At first, they will not talk to her, but one of the prison guards knows Mama from doing laundry for his wife. He follows her outside and says our Papa is being held for questioning. Everyday, Mama goes to prison with food. Soldiers take her food, but guards will not let her see our Papa. My sisters Sophie and Anna, my baby brother Levi, and I cry all the time. Five weeks pass, and just when we think we will never see him again, Papa shows up at our doorstep. We cannot believe how he looks. Our Papa is like a bag of bones. His eyes are sunken into his head, and it looks like he has not eaten in a very long time. It is as though he does not know us. Mama tries to fatten him up with her special soups, but Papa is not same man. At night I would bury my head under my blanket and cover little Levi's ears with my hands when Papa would scream out terror in his dreams. He was only home for a week when he got a terrible fever. Mama called Rabbi Solomon to say the special prayers for the sick. Papa just lay in bed for five days. I remember that I was foolishly happy that he wasn't screaming anymore at night. Then, on the fifth day, he just slipped away in his sleep."

"Why did the soldiers do this?"

"It is much same story everywhere with our people. The Jews in Russia have all time been mistreated. But it became very bad in the seventeen-hundreds under a ruler called Ivan the Terrible. Then Catherine the Great came along about a hundred years later and forced all Jews from their villages to go live in special areas of the land. This lady ruler was not so *great* for my people. But to answer your question, maybe my papa was unlucky, or maybe he was tortured because, Papa was Jewish and married Mama."

"What do ya mean?"

"Mama is cousin to Czar Nicholas. She is a Romanov. Her family deserted her when she fell in love with my papa."

"Is your mother a Jew?"

"No, Mama is Catholic, but with respect to Papa, she honors ways of his people. Mama says that all Christians, Muslims, and Jews have the same God and follow the same rule. Doc Simpson said you call it *Golden Rule*. We have same rule in the Torah and it is also in the Muslim book called Koran. Mama says, at the heart of it, all people are the same. If each of us will respect this rule there will never be need to hate." For some reason the image of Bull came into Otto's head.

Chandler remembered that although his parents weren't exactly church-going folks, they were always reminding him to follow the *Golden Rule* and do unto others as you would like others to do unto you. "It's a good rule, Otto."

Chandler glanced at Otto and the unusual leather bag he wore across his shoulder. "Say, I've been meaning to ask. Tell me about that bottle you carry inside this bag you always have at your side?" he asked pointing to the leather sack. "I've seen you gazing at it when you think no one is looking."

Otto reached for the bag and touched it with his hand. He thought of how much the Amethyst Bottle reminded him of his mother and how it gave him comfort to gaze at it. The cautious part of him did not want to share the bottle, but on the other hand, he liked Chandler and knew that the ten-year-old boy was just being curious.

"It is just a bottle," Otto muttered hoping to discourage his friend.

"Can I see it?" Chandler persisted with the doggedness of a ten-year-old.

Otto thought of the special amethyst crest hidden under his shirt, which he had not shared with anyone since the night Esther had placed the bottle into his hands at Doc Simpson's office. He looked into the hopeful eyes of his friend and reluctantly said, "I guess so. But just to look. It is made of a kind of glass, and I would not want to break it." Otto carefully pulled the Amethyst Bottle from its sack and held it out for Chandler to view.

Chandler gazed at the colorful little bottle. "What a pretty color!" Chandler remarked pointing a particular shade of purple on the bottle. "It reminds me of the purple Iris's Ma used to grow along the front of our farmhouse back home. When the bulbs popped up through the soil, we all knew that spring was on its way. I used to love to see the flowers sway in the breeze. Where'd ya get it?"

The cautious part of Otto hesitated. "Um...it was given to me by a very nice lady a few week's before coming out west. Most of time, I use it for storing water. It is special gift. I think it will bring me good fortune."

Chandler stroked the bottle with his hand thinking it might bring him some fortune. "I hope you're right. You've sure been through a lot. Seems to me, you need a little luck. I don't know what I'd do if I were taken away from my folks."

Otto looked back at the wagons and saw Victoria picking wildflowers as she walked alone. "Say, what is matter with your sister, Chandler? I have try to talk to her, but she just stiffens up. I don't think she likes me."

"Oh, that's just her way. Victoria's sort of shy. You gotta give her time to get to know you. You see, my sister missed a lot of school being sickly the last few winters with a bad cough. She's just a little quiet 'cause of never being around too many people. It's funny though, since being on the trail, she seems happier."

Otto glanced down at the bottle and felt gentle warmth spreading onto his hands. It seemed to radiate from the Amethyst Bottle. But that made no sense. Otto knitted his brow. He wondered if the heat was a result of the bottle being exposed to the rays of the sun, or if it was something else. The sensation warmed his hands, and gave him a feeling of comfort much like when Mama used to tuck him into bed on a cold winter's night. Otto carefully placed the bottle back into its case, but a kernel of an idea began to pop into his head.

Chapter 6 ~ May 1854 - Alcove Spring

Ghost Walker moved through his world like a coyote clinging to the shadows of night. Although he was grateful to Captain McAuliffe for taking him on as a scout, he never felt as though he belonged in the white-man's world. But because his people were gone, and he had no where else to go, Ghost Walker made the best of it by working hard for the kind man who had saved his life. If McAuliffe noticed that the Indian had pulled back from being the inquisitive young Indian he had come to know on their first wagon train together, he never mentioned it.

Over the years, Ghost Walker had come to learn that most of the people who traveled west on the wagon trains seemed either in awe or frightened of him. Rarely did they try to get to know him, but he also knew he was difficult to get to know. Mostly people just left him to himself. McAuliffe's man, Bull, had at times been downright ornery to Ghost Walker, and on several occasions, the pair had almost come to blows. But most of the time, the scout found it prudent to ignore him. The loneliest times came when he noticed a pioneer's furtive pair of eyes boring into him with distain. These looks made the Indian feel as though he just didn't belong – anywhere.

Ghost Walker appreciated that the wagon master respected his privacy. Yet, when they did exchange ideas, the brave noted that McAuliffe treated him with the kindness of a father. The Indian had been somewhat surprised when Mac asked him to teach the Russian boy how to ride a horse. Later he would wonder if the captain had a shadowy motive for placing the two in each other's path, but at the time, he had only nodded his head to show that he would honor the request.

Ghost Walker had not wanted to become friendly with Otto, but it was hard not to like the boy. Otto had been so pleased to learn how to ride that he talked the Indian's ear off with questions about horses and riding in general. Over time, the scout found himself telling Otto more about his life than any other white person, including McAuliffe.

It was a crisp clear afternoon and Ghost Walker had taken Otto riding. They stopped to water the horses at a creek so cold and pure that Otto thought it must have come from melting snow somewhere in the distance. In truth, it originated from an underground spring over a mile away. Otto breathed in the air with delight as he viewed the sheer vastness of the prairie. He thought the spot was beautiful and felt somewhat sad when, at length, Ghost Walker guided their horses away from the area.

"What is the name of your horse, Ghost Walker?"

The Indian looked away from Otto, and for a moment the boy thought he might not answer. "Little Feather," the brave reluctantly volunteered. Otto thought the words rolled off the Indian's tongue like the whispering sound of the wind.

"It is good name. I think it must be because of mark on pony's forehead. I see it that first day we go riding. It looks just like a small feather floating in the wind."

Ghost Walker patted his pony's neck and nodded. "Not many people see likeness in this mark, but you are right, Otto."

Otto noticed that, for an instant, a cloud seemed to pass over the Indian's face.

For the past weeks, as the two boys had inched toward companionship, Otto slowly began to share the details of his family and how he came to work as a horse wrangler on the wagon train. In time, Ghost Walker found that the paths of their lives were somewhat alike. Both were alone and without family, and both were most comfortable speaking in the language of their youth.

What's more, the Indian came to appreciate that Otto seemed genuinely interested in learning about his people. He began by asking Ghost Walker what various English words meant in the Lakota language of the Sioux. At first, Ghost Walker translated the words of his people merely to pass the time as they took their daily riding lessons during the *nooning* meal – a time when most people ate and rested up for the long afternoon march. But, over time, Otto had completely surprised Ghost Walker by remembering nearly all of the pleasant-sounding words of the Sioux.

Otto had only recently come to realize that he seemed to have a special gift for languages. He enjoyed the challenge of the way the new sounds rolled off his tongue. So, he continued learning more Lakota words from the Indian until they could, in fact, carry on simple conversations.

Lately, Ghost Walker found that he actually looked forward to the riding lessons – if that is what one could call their outings. In truth, Ghost Walker knew that Otto was now as comfortable on a horse as any capable rider. But each afternoon, the two companions headed away from the wagon train to scout what was up ahead and learn more words of his people. For Ghost Walker, it felt strangely comforting to converse in the language of his parents.

"*Tokaho?* What's wrong, Ghost Walker?"

Ghost Walker looked into the distant grass and saw three crows pecking at the remains of a dead rabbit. "*Kangi,*" muttered the Indian as he shuddered.

"What about the crow?"

Ghost Walker grunted. "Me not care for *kangi.*" Ghost Walker turned his attention away from the crows and looked to the sky. "*Wayanka*! Look! There in sky! *Wambli*. Now that is fine bird."

Otto agreed that the eagle was indeed a noble bird. Instinctively, he rubbed his hand across his chest to make sure he felt the outline of his crest of an eagle with two heads. He looked at Ghost Walker sitting astride the pretty pony named Little Feather and admired the beautiful arrowhead that the scout had fashioned into a necklace with rawhide and beads. Otto knew that, like himself, the Indian never took the rawhide band off. But unlike Otto's crest, Ghost Walker's necklace was worn in plain view for all to see. Otto resisted the temptation to share his crest with the Indian.

"Tell me about *tatanka*, Ghost Walker."

"*Ohan*, Otto." Ghost Walker knew that it was hard to resist the enthusiasm of the boy. "To Sioux, buffalo is gift of all life. *Tatanka* move in great herds with so many bulls, cows, and young walking together that the dust from their hooves can be seen for long distance. *Tatanka* is grazing animal but they have problem. Can only see with sharp eye at close range. *Tatanka* no match when Sioux braves ride with wind on their fine ponies with spears and arrows. After hunt there is always dancing and great feasting to give thanks to Mother Earth for her blessings. Our people use every part of *tatanka* to help us in our daily lives."

As the two companions lazily rode their horses across the prairie, they were so engrossed in Ghost Walker's praise of the bison that they did not notice a lone mountain lion lurking in the grass.

The mountain lion was old and had not eaten for many days. Even small rabbits and squirrels had been able to outwit the old warrior. The cougar possessed several lesions on his face – each injury a battle scar from his youthful days when he was strong and could pounce and leap with the fury of a storm. One of his eyes drooped low from an old injury from the claw of a bear. He had barely escaped with his life that time, and he was nearly blind in that eye. The ancient mountain lion's body was covered in ticks, and his fur was matted and dirty. He knew that if he did not eat, his days would soon be over. The lion looked at the two large horses walking slowly across the prairie in his direction, but his attention was focused on the riders. The ancient warrior hoped to startle the larger animals so that they would rear up and drop the smaller animals to the grass. Instinct would take over, and the old lion would pounce on the weaker prey. He would go for the neck and cut off the supply of air to the heart. It would be over swiftly. His prey would feel little pain. The old mountain lion's stomach grumbled with hunger, but years of practice as a skilled hunter told him to lie still and use the yellow grass as cover. The experienced cat knew that he was positioned down wind from the animals and they would not be able to smell his scent.

"Ghost Walker, tell me about the arrowhead you wear around your neck."

The Indian reached up and tenderly covered the stone with his hand and then patted his stomach. "*Lowacin*, Otto. We head back to wagon train. Story must wait for another day."

Otto tugged on the reins of his horse and thought, *I'm hungry too.* Otto gently pulled the reins to one side to turn his horse back in the direction of the wagon train when he saw something moving in the grass out of the corner of his eye. But it was too late.

At that moment, both horses reared up and whinnied. Loud screeching noises resonated from the panicky horses, and the riders struggled to hang on. Ghost Walker gripped his thighs tightly to the back of his pony as his horse bolted across the prairie. "*Sunkawakan*! Crazy horse! Slow down!" he yelled.

Otto was not as fortunate. He was thrown to the ground while his terrified horse sprinted in the direction of the wagon train. Otto folded his limbs into his body and tumbled like a stone for a few feet before he came to rest on his knees. Terror gripped his body as the cat sprang out of the grass toward him.

Otto might have been dead, but the old mountain lion's eyes betrayed him. As he leapt toward his prey, he overshot his mark, and he too tumbled into a summersault before landing several yards from his victim. The mountain lion was dazed and his muscles ached from the thrust of his attack, but he rose to his feet and stared at the boy on his knees in the grass. The cougar could smell fear from his victim. He knew that his prey was now in a vulnerable position, and that he held the advantage. With measured steps, the old lion closed the gap between him and his next meal.

Otto searched frantically in the grass for a weapon – something to give him a fighting chance against the three-hundred pound beast. In his frantic effort, Otto's hand grazed against the leather satchel holding the Amethyst Bottle. Instinct took over as he thrust his hands to his side. In one blazing motion, Otto removed the leather strap from his neck. He used the strap to swing the bottle in a fast circular motion.

The lion stopped only for a second to look at the swirling motion of the object before he decided to pounce. At that moment, Otto let go of the strap and the bottle hit the charging lion square between the eyes. To the young boy's astonishment, the old mountain lion dropped to the grass like a boulder, and the bottle glanced off its target and came to rest innocently in the grass.

Otto looked at the cat slumped in the grass at his knees. He sat frozen in fear and did not hear Ghost Walker ride up and slip off his horse. The Indian knelt down and placed his hand on the neck of the cat. "*Igmu* is dead," he said in awe. The Indian surveyed the animal with respect. "This cat very old. Live long time. Otto make good kill. Ancestors very proud of young brave. Bring honor to family."

Otto remembered the bottle. His legs were like rubber, and as much as he tried, he could not force his limbs into a standing position. He looked at Ghost Walker, and the Indian picked Otto up with the ease of someone who might pick up a pillow, and moved the boy a several yards away from the fallen predator. He gently set Otto on the yellow grass. Otto's heart felt like it was pounding outside his chest. He pointed but could only force one word out of his mouth. "Bottle."

Ghost Walker nodded at his young friend. He ambled over to the bottle resting near the lion and brought it to the boy.

Frantically, Otto untied the leather cord and removed the bottle from its case. His hands moved over every section of the bottle until he was satisfied that it had not been chipped or cracked. Otto let out a huge sigh and looked at Ghost Walker.

"Thank you," he whispered.

The Sioux Indian nodded solemnly. "Ghost Walker hold bottle?"

"Of course."

Ghost Walker cradled the bottle respectfully in his hands. For an instant, Otto thought he saw some of the tired creases fade from around his eyes. "I see Otto drink from this bottle many times and give much thought to its beautiful color. Color of bottle brings picture to my head. I see me as young boy gazing in wonder at mountains of my land – the Dakotas. Each autumn, when cottonwood leaves turn yellow, a strange vision comes to pass. Just as sun set in western sky, mountains in east turn the color of flowering sage – color of your bottle. This is signal to our people that it is time to gather our things and leave open lands for safety of mountains. We spend our winters away from howling winds that sweep across prairie. We live quietly inside warmth of our tipis among tall trees and listen to old men tell stories of our ancestors. We cut strong branches from trees to make new lodge poles for summer homes."

Ghost Walker sighed. "Color of bottle reminds me of strange trick autumn sun played on our eyes – to cast this paint across the mountains at end of day. It was sign that beautiful color was calling us home to higher ground. I did not think something so pretty would also make good weapon. Good thinking, Otto."

Ghost Walker slowly handed the bottle back to Otto and grunted. "There is powerful medicine in this bottle. Bottle carry strong spirit into my hands." Ghost Walker looked into Otto's eyes and uttered, "Otto must guard this bottle well."

"Thank you, Ghost Walker. I will."

Otto and Ghost Walker stayed near the fallen lion for another half hour before Ghost Walker suggested that it was time to head back to the wagon train.

"What about the lion?"

"*Igmu* live honorable life. Tonight he will give himself to wolves or perhaps a pack of coyotes. Then buzzards will take their turn. In his passing, he will help others live another day. This is as it should be. This is Mother Earth's plan for the way we live."

Ghost Walker helped pull Otto up behind him so that Little Feather could carry them back to the wagon train.

"What about my horse?" asked Otto.

"Horse find his way back to wagon train. Otto not to worry."

Ghost Walker positioned Otto in back of him and nudged the horse in the direction of the wagon train. They rode in silence for a few minutes until the scout cleared his throat and remarked, "Today, my brother Otto, make Ghost Walker very proud."

Otto's heart opened to the word *brother*, and he asked, "Ghost Walker?"

"Yes, Otto."

"I want to tell you a story from a very old book called the Old Testament. I think you may like it." If Otto could have seen the Indian's face, he would have enjoyed the traces of a grin spreading across the mouth of the scout. He also would have been surprised and saddened to know that it was the first time the Indian had smiled in a very long time. Instead, he only saw the back of Ghost Walker's head nod up and down – the signal for Otto to begin his tale.

"Once, a long time ago, there was a boy named David. He was quite small compared to this other large giant of a man named Goliath, but David was not afraid...."

Chapter 7 ~ May 1854 - Platte River

The wagon train had been traveling west beside the Platte River for two days. Otto sat astride a sturdy brown Quarter Horse that had come up lame about a week ago and looked at the sun dancing across the surface of the river. He was surprised when McAuliffe rode up beside him and slowed his horse to match the gate of Otto's horse.

"How's the horse?" the captain asked as he pulled out his bag of tobacco.

"Good. A week walking behind with the cow column seems to have been just the rest he needed."

"It looks as though the riding lessons from Ghost Walker have been a success. You sit in the saddle like you were born to it, Otto. How are you two getting along?"

"Thanks, Captain McAuliffe. Ghost Walker is good teacher. We are *getting along* much like brothers now. I learn many things from him."

McAuliffe smiled and nodded his head. "I know. I've learned a few things from him myself. That's just what I was hoping to hear, Otto. Ghost Walker has not had an easy road to bear. I'm happy that you two are enjoying each other's company."

"What does this mean? Did Ghost Walker find bear in road?"

McAuliffe let out a loud roar of laughter. "I'm sorry, Otto. What I mean is Ghost Walker has not had an easy life. I found him almost dead on the prairie when he was about your age. His family had been wiped out by some soldiers or an enemy tribe.

He has been scarred deeply. I'm happy that you two have warmed to each other."

Otto squinted his eyes and opened his mouth to speak, but was cut off by the captain.

"Sorry Otto. Let me say that again. I'm happy that you two have become friends."

Otto looked across at the man who had agreed to take him out west and said, "I cannot find words to say thanks for giving me work. I like my job. Mama will be so happy to know I have learned to ride. Out here, I see so many things I never witness before."

"I've seen you writing in your journal, Otto. It's important that you record what you see. I feel that what we're doing settling the wilderness is important for our country. You'll enjoy reading your book to your children when you're an old man like me."

Otto wondered if the captain was teasing him because, except for his occasional coughing spells, he looked strong and fit and didn't seem old at all.

"Take this river for instance." McAuliffe pointed to the Platte. "We'd never be able to make this trip west if it weren't for the Platte River."

"How is this?" Otto asked.

"Well, most of the big rivers in America run north and south – like the Mighty Mississippi and the Colorado River out west, but the Platte River runs east and west for about five hundred miles. Another great river called the Missouri lies north of here. Two brave explorers, Lewis Merriweather and James Clark, led a small band of men all the way to the Pacific Ocean following its path. They called themselves the Corp of Discovery, and they were the first white men to explore our great land all the way to the Pacific Ocean. We owe much to their discovery of new plants and animals, and the maps they made on their journey."

McAuliffe pointed to the river. "By following the shores of the Platte, we not only have plenty of water for us and our livestock, we know it's taking us in the general direction of where we want to go. This river will take us to Fort Laramie and then on to Independence Rock. Things will begin to get a might more interesting after that."

Otto was not sure what the captain meant by *interesting*, but he thought he would just be patient and trust that the captain would safely guide them to California. Otto said, "It will be good to see new land. This land is too much the same. Sometimes I feel like we walk but we do not move."

Captain McAuliffe laughed. "I know, Otto. But there'll come a time when we'll all wish the going was as easy as traveling alongside the waters of the Platte.

"Might I ask question, Captain?"

"Ask away, Otto."

"You have interesting name, but I am very much curious. What does "P" stand for in your name?"

Cornelius P. McAuliffe let out a roar of laughter. "Now that son is indeed an interesting question, but one I rarely discuss." Mac looked fondly at the youth and softened. "Maybe later. You take care now, Otto, and let me know if you have need of anything. Let's ride, Dickens"

The wagon master tapped his heels against the side of his horse. Otto watched in confusion as the captain rode Dickens up the line to catch up with Ghost Walker who was riding at the head of the train.

Victoria Dickerson was happier than she had ever been in her life. The thirteen-year-old felt that she was finally on an adventure. Back home, she spent most of her days cooped up in the family's log cabin sitting under a pile of blankets reading books, and taking endless spoonfuls of disgusting tonic which was supposed to ease her coughing spells and make her stronger. She loved reading, but she always felt like she was a girl on the outside looking in. But now, for the first time in her young life, she wasn't just reading books about young heroines like Joan of Arc who was a champion for the French people – or a brave young princess who was captured by a band of pirates for ransom, only to be rescued by a handsome prince. She was heading west with the other pioneers who made up the wagon train, and Victoria felt she was not just reading about an adventure – she was on one!

Victoria loved her parents, but they had always been so protective of her when they had lived on the farm in Springfield, Illinois. Now, Tony and Julia Dickerson were so occupied with the day to day tasks of keeping their wagon rolling and keeping the family fed, they seemed far too busy to watch her every move. Young Victoria was allowed to walk alongside the train when the weather was nice and pick wildflowers to press between the pages of her books, or to watch the prairie sunrises or changing cloud formations. Already, she had been astounded by some of the sights she had seen. Like the band of twenty Indians that had been following their train for three days. These people were not like Ghost Walker or other Indians she had seen around her home in Illinois.

This wretched band of men, women and children seemed to depend solely on wagon trains for their livelihood. They had no horses and Victoria observed that they walked behind the wagons at a distance of about two hundred yards. They were easy to spot because of their unusual and brightly-colored clothing. The Indians almost looked as though they were dressed for a fancy ball. Victoria had learned about them from the captain two nights ago when he brought the members together for a meeting.

McAuliffe had said, "Sometimes a few Indians find it appealing to split off from their tribe and follow the allure of the wagon trains. They see white folks with items that are new and unusual to them and they think that these things are important to have. Sadly, these scavengers live off the discarded wares of the pioneers and are there to pick up cast-off items. So, they tag behind, like buzzards, hoping to snatch up something from a pioneer who has decided that he can live without it to lighten the load for his oxen. The groups will follow the wagon trains looking for food and clothes or other interesting trinkets." McAuliffe had cautioned the members to stand extra guard at night until the Indians got tired of tagging behind their group. "They're harmless enough for the most part, but a hat or a shiny copper pot might come up missing while you're asleep if you're not careful."

Victoria noticed that the distribution of the clothes among these Indians appeared to be all mixed up. It was strange to see men proudly swagger along in ladies' silk dresses and brightly colored bonnets with fancy bows. One old man, who looked to be the chief of the rag-tag band, actually wore a copper bowl on his head. Victoria thought the metal must have gotten awfully hot as it pressed against his skull in the heat of the midday sun, but he seemed delighted with the way it complimented his blue and red waistcoat and pink silk petticoat. When bacon became too rancid to eat or beans turned too sour for the pioneers, the items were tossed by the side of the road. Victoria would see the women race to the objects like a pack of coyotes and snatch the food up. When the train stopped for the nooning meal, the Indians did likewise, and a fire was quickly made to cook up the spoiled food. If someone got sick, that person would just step off to the side, throw-up, and then jog back to their spot on the trail hardly without losing a beat.

At sunset, Otto carried a bucket down to the river to fetch some water for Biscuit. As he filled it, he saw Victoria sitting on a rock dangling her feet in the shallow shores of the river as she held her nose in a book. The day had been hot and muggy and the water looked cool on her toes. Otto noticed Chandler setting out some traps to catch catfish twenty yards or so down river. Otto looked over at the girl and decided that this might be the perfect opportunity to stir up some conversation on an idea he had been hatching since his encounter with the mountain lion. He picked up the pail of water, adjusted the bottle at his side, drew in a breath and strode over to where she sat. *If I can meet head-on with a mountain lion, I can face a girl!*

"Good evening," he ventured.

Victoria looked up from her book and smiled shyly. "Hello, Otto."

"Nice weather tonight."

"Yes." Victoria looked around and added, "I like the way the days are stretching out and the nights are shrinking shorter. There is so much more time to read." With that, Victoria turned her attention back to her book.

Otto coughed. "I agree. In fact, I come to talk to you about this very thing."

"What's that, Otto?" Victoria said without looking up.

"Well, it is just that I want to make a trade with you."

Victoria pulled her head up from the book and looked at Otto. "What trade, Otto? What item do you want to trade with me?"

"A book. I mean I want to trade for a book. I am learning to read in English from my Bible, and I so very much want to …well…borrow a book."

Victoria looked directly into the face of Otto and stared at him in wonder.

"Blue with little specks of lavender around the edges," Otto declared.

Victoria glared at Otto as if was crazy. "What are you talking about?"

"Oh! Sorry, it is your eyes. I finally see that they are blue… with little specks of lavender…." Otto's voice trailed off, thinking that he sounded like an idiot.

"What does the color of my eyes have to do with trading for a book, Otto?"

"Nothing. It is just that I have been wondering what color your eyes might be, but I never see because you are always looking down into book. Sorry. I am just stupid Russian boy with brain of a weasel."

Victoria looked at Otto for a few seconds and then burst into laughter. She laughed so hard that tears welled up inside the blue eyes with lavender specks around the edges.

Otto was embarrassed with humiliation. In anger, he turned to leave but tripped over the pail of water he had set in the grass and fell. As he lay face down in the grass, he wished he could become a worm and burrow into the earth forever.

In an instant, Victoria was kneeling by his prone body. "I'm terribly sorry, Otto. Are you hurt?"

Otto shook his head but did not look at Victoria as he struggled to get up from the ground. He was about to stand up when Victoria grabbed hold of his arm.

"Please forgive me. I can see that I hurt your feelings. I didn't mean to...I mean I was not laughing at *you*...only at what you said about the weasel. I think you're terribly funny. It's just that I don't always know what to say around other people because I've spent a lot of time alone. Sometimes my words just come out wrong."

Otto looked down at the hand on his arm and sat back down on the grass. "It is alright. Same thing happens to me. Only it is because I am just learning English and I know sometimes I say words wrong. I am always told so by Bull. He likes to make fun of me. He says...when I put foot in mouth."

Victoria laughed. "See there you are again making me laugh. Let's start all over again. Good evening, Otto. It's so nice to see you this fine evening."

"It is pleasure for me, Victoria."

The two companions looked at each other for a few seconds and then they both started to laugh. Victoria sat on the grass across from Otto and said, "Now, what's this trade you wish to make with me for a book. I will be happy to loan you any book I have. There is no need to trade for one."

"This is most kind of you, but I have something that I think you might like to see. I think that you would do well to trade for it."

Otto slowly untied the top of his leather bag and carefully pulled the Amethyst Bottle from its case. "See. This is special gift given to me, and I would like to share it with you."

Victoria looked at the bottle in wonder. "Oh, Otto, this bottle is charming. The purple colors are astonishing." Victoria pointed to a section of the bottle. "This shade of violet reminds me of a ribbon I once wore when I was eight. Mama was buying some kitchen items from a traveling salesman. He was a funny little sprite of a man with rosy cheeks and a twinkle in his eye. I stood near Mama clinging shyly to her skirts looking in wonder at all the fancy gadgets hanging from inside his wagon. When the bargaining was over, the salesman looked directly at me and said that he had something very special – fit for a princess. I watched in wonder as he cut a yard of the most unusual color of violet ribbon from a large spool and twirled the strip in the air. And then he let the ribbon go with a flourish and a wink, and it gently floated into my hands. I had never seen a satin ribbon in that particular shade of purple. I cherished that pretty strip of satin as if it were spun gold and wore it in my hair everyday for a year." Victoria knitted her brow and continued.

"Then one day, I was helping Mama take the clothes off the line because we could see there was a big storm brewing to the west. My heart became crushed when a strong gust of wind snatched the ribbon clean off my head. I caught my breath as the beautiful strand of satin danced upward in the wind like the tail of a kite. I wanted to run and chase it, but just then a crack of lightening splintered in the sky, and Mama grabbed my hand and pulled me and the laundry basket into the safety of the house. I cried that night over the silly ribbon, but Mama told me not to worry because she'd get me another the next time the salesman passed our way. But that curious little man never came back by our farm. Mama tried to talk me into other ribbons when we'd be shopping in town, but I never saw another one even close to that shade of violet so I told her *we'd wait*. Then I got sick that winter and somehow I just forgot about the ribbon." Victoria looked down at the Amethyst Bottle and sighed. "You know, it's funny how something can instantly remind you of another thing. I never expected to see that exact color again, yet here it is in your bottle." The girl sighed wistfully and said, "How odd, I hadn't thought of that ribbon in years."

Victoria suddenly looked embarrassed and handed the bottle back to Otto. "Goodness, Otto. Listen to me. Chattering on like a mockingbird at sunrise. I don't know what has gotten into me. I usually don't talk much at all. I'm sorry."

Otto pushed the bottle back into Victoria's hands. "Don't be sorry, Victoria. I like to hear you talk. I think this bottle likes you! If you would be so kind to take it for a few hours each day, a huge problem would be solved for both of us. You could help me with my reading, and my bottle could be with you."

Victoria wanted to laugh again, but bit her lip to stop the impulse. "Otto, a bottle doesn't want to *be* with a particular person. It can't *like* someone. Only another living thing can do that, and anyway, I will be more than happy to help you with your reading. You do not have to loan me your bottle." Victoria sighed as she looked at the bottle. "It *is* lovely though."

"Victoria. Let me see. How can I say this? This bottle is not like other bottles. It is very special. It was given to me by a kind lady named Esther, and she said the strength within this bottle will help me on my journey. I think this special bottle will help you too."

"What ever do you mean?" Victoria asked defensively, "Do you think I need help?"

"No, no, but I have seen you cough, and I believe *this* bottle might help you to feel better. How can I explain? Let me think. Can you see these words on the bottom of the bottle?"

"Yes. The words look like they're in Latin."

"Yes, yes, words are in Latin. Esther told me that words say:

> *Into thy hand I come,*
> *Unto thy spirit as one.*

"But what does that have to do with me?"

"I am thinking that bottle may be good for coughing. You do not have to take, but it would give me great pleasure if you might try this for me. I have not much to give for such a kind

73

deed as you would be doing to teach me in the reading. It would make me very happy to share gift of this bottle with you."

Victoria looked at Otto with a bemused stare and then thought, *What harm could come of this?* "Well, if that is what you want, Otto, it will be my pleasure to *borrow* your bottle for a few hours each day."

Otto was overjoyed until he noticed the bucket of spilt water near his feet. "Oh, I must get back to camp with water or Biscuit might come looking for me with dirty frying pan," Otto joked.

Victoria handed the pretty bottle back to Otto and smiled at him from eyes that were blue with lavender specks around the edges. We'll start tomorrow, and. . .well thanks, Otto."

Chapter 8 ~ June 1854 - North Platte River

Sunday, tenth day of June

Dearest Mama,

I continue to write to you in English to practice my letters. A few days ago we passed a place called Chimney Rock which looked like the steeple on a church. Many people tried to climb it, but with little success. We have been following the Platte River for several weeks. It split into a fork and Captain McAuliffe safely showed us where to cross to what is now called the North Platte. This will take us in to Fort Laramie where we will rest for several days.

I have finally made a friend with the girl named Victoria, and she has loaned me a dictionary to help me with my spelling. Each day, after I go riding with Ghost Walker, I have reading lessons with Victoria. The English words come easy for me now and we mostly spend our time talking about the characters in the books and what the author had in mind when the plot goes in a particular direction. We just finished a story called Jane Eyre by an English woman named Charlotte Bronte. It is about a poor orphan girl who grows up to become a governess for a rich lord. It was a good tale and kept my attention all the way to the end. It is sad to know there are a lot of people with different troubles in life, but it makes me feel not so alone. A book I like even better is by the American author James Fennimore Cooper. His novel, The Last of the Mohicans, is filled with adventures about a scout named Hawkeye and his faithful Mohican friend, Uncas, as they fight against the French and another tribe of Indians.

Speaking of adventures, I feel as though I am part of one. I have seen so many new things. We are heading to Fort Laramie and I for one will be so happy to get there. Captain McAuliffe says that we will spend a week there resting the livestock and storing up on supplies. The mood of the members is low, but I know that spirits will rise again after the long rest at the fort. It will be nice to see a change from the flat earth of the prairie country.

You will never believe what the people in the wagon train use to fuel the campfires! Since there are not many trees on the prairie, the children run around and collect buffalo chips. These dried rounds of grassy manure produce a hearty fire with no smelly flavor added to the food.

The other day I was out riding with Ghost Walker, and I saw a sight that will never leave my memory. There in the distance, we saw a herd of buffalo so large that there were too many to count. Scores of tatanka (this is the Sioux word for buffalo taught to me by my friend Ghost Walker) blacken the grassy prairie, and this vast open land that the pioneers are hoping to tame! It stretches as far as the eye can see until it touches a sky so clear and blue it makes a person feel humble and small. I feel sorry for the Indians who make this place their home. Ghost Walker has told me wonderful stories about the customs of his people, but he is afraid that the time of the Sioux and all tribes may be coming to an end.

I must go return a book to Victoria but I will write again of my adventures soon.

Your devoted son, Otto Stanoff

Otto walked over to the Dickerson's' camp just as they were finishing Sunday breakfast. Mrs. Dickerson looked tired as she stood washing the tin cups and plates. It hadn't rained in two weeks and Otto noticed that a thick layer of dust covered the canvas of their wagon. Otto had long since observed that a steady breeze blew in from the west, but lately the wind felt different. When there was no moisture in the ground the wind stirred up dust which settled on people's clothes and got into the creases around the eyes and up their noses. Otto knew that, like Mrs. Dickerson, the other members of the train were weary from travel and a little edgy from the constant swirl of dust. Otto was happiest when he could walk off to one side or amble out in front of the train. If he strayed a might too far off the trail, he knew that the cloud of dust stirred from the hooves of the oxen and horses ensured that he could safely make his way back to the train.

Otto walked up to Victoria to return the book of poems by Ralph Waldo Emerson. Victoria flashed Otto a huge smile before walking over to the wagon to place the book back into her trunk.

"How are you today, Mrs. Dickerson?"

Julia Dickerson looked at Otto and said, "It is Sunday, Otto, and my flesh is happy for a day away from the dust, and jarring of the wagon. I'm fixing to rest a might, but first I have some mending to do for Jessica and Christina." Julia looked at Otto and spoke softly, "Say, I've had a hankering to talk to you about something." Mrs. Dickerson looked in the direction of the wagon then turned back to the boy. "Otto, I don't know what's inside that cherished bottle of yours, but ever since Julia's been carrying it around in the afternoons, well...she just looks healthier than I've ever seen her in years. When she first told me that you believed the bottle would help her with her coughing, well...I just smiled and inwardly shook my head. But to be honest, it seems as though she breathes easier these days, and I haven't heard a squeak of a cough outta her in weeks. It may just all be a coincidence, but just in case it ain't, I just want to say thanks for what you've done for her."

"It is not my doing Mrs. Dickerson. It is truly this special bottle." Otto patted it at his side. "Julia helped me too with the reading. I like to discuss with her the things that I read. She is so smart. I think she makes me smart too. Good day, ma'am."

Julia Dickerson chuckled at Otto's candid remarks and turned her attention to her dishes as Victoria and Otto greeted each other. Then something made her stop. She looked at the pair walking away from the wagon. "You two be careful and don't stray off too far from the wagon train. The sky looks funny like it might rain."

Otto nodded, then looked over at Chandler who was watching his dad repair the yoke on one of the harnesses of the oxen and called over his shoulder, "Chandler, would you like to come?"

"Naw. You two will just gab on about poetry or some passage from a book. Anyway, I need to help Pa with some odd jobs. I'll catch up with ya later to set out some fish traps."

Otto nodded his head and waved goodbye as he and Victoria headed away from the camp. Remembering his recent conversation with Mrs. Dickerson, Otto removed the bottle from his shoulder and handed it to Victoria. She smiled at him and carefully placed the strap over her shoulder.

"Ma thinks the bottle is helping me breathe better."

"What do you think?"

"I don't quite know for certain, but I like carrying it. I think...mostly because it's yours." Victoria turned away shyly and added, "I will admit that I don't seem to wake up coughing in the night and that gets me a better night's sleep."

Otto thought the cool morning air felt heavy like having one too many blankets on top of you at night. The sky was not the usual clear blue, but possessed a haze that made the horizon appear to be an odd yellowish-green color. Otto dismissed the thought from his mind. He was happy to get away from the bustle of the wagon train and spend time with his friend. He decided to take Victoria to a place that he and Ghost Walker had scouted out early that morning. They had discovered a rather large island in the middle of the Platte River with a few trees growing on its soil. He told Victoria how odd it was to see a stand of trees on the island, but nary a one on the shores of the Platte.

The pair had been walking for thirty minutes when Otto said, "Thanks for the loan of the book, Victoria."

"You're welcome. Was there one poem that stood out to you, Otto?"

"I really liked the one called *The Concord Hymn*."

"Oh, that's one of my favorites. What did you like about it?"

"Well, I liked the way the local farmers stood on the arched bridge to face their foe, which I guess was the British army at the start of the Revolutionary War."

"Yes, that's right. The poem was written to honor the men who fought there."

Otto spoke. "And because of their bravery Mr. Emerson wrote that, *a shot was heard around the world.* For me, I like to think that the author wrote that particular line as an encouragement to other nations that are governed by unkind rulers. The poem gives me hope that common folks might stand together and do what they feel is right if they are mistreated." Otto thought of his own people and the way they had been forced by Catherine the Great to leave their land and go live in an area where *she* felt they should live.

"You're right again, Otto, and our founding fathers thought so too. Why just last year, I heard a man in Springfield address that very thing in our town hall. He had recently served in the United States Congress. He was a tall man with dark features and went by the name of Abraham Lincoln. He was by no means a handsome man, but there was something about him."

"What do you mean?"

"Well, he just had a way about him – a twinkle in his eye, and he told wonderful stories. But, the thing I remember most was him telling us that our founding fathers took great pains when they framed the constitution to insure that religion would be kept separate from the way our country is run. He stirred up different feelings in the group when he said, *As a nation we began by declaring that 'all men are created equal.'* He went on to say that it's dead wrong to think, *all men are created equal except Negroes and foreigners.*

Not everyone agreed with him, of course, but that's what's great about our country. We have the right to think differently.

He moved me, and I agree with his message. I know I would not want to live in a country run by kings and dictators. Mr. Lincoln said that what's remarkable about America is that any common man, like himself, can be voted into office by his peers, because that's what our founding fathers meant when they wrote in the Declaration of Independence of having a country *of the people, by the people, and for the people."*

"I like this saying. I also like this man called Abraham, which I should add, is a fine Hebrew name from the Old Testament. I think your Mr. Lincoln sounds very wise. You know, Victoria, I like your country so much, I believe I'd like to stay here, and one day bring Mama and Sophie and Anna and little Levi here. But first, I must find Ivan."

Victoria looked across at her friend and smiled. Suddenly, she stopped. Otto saw her skin turn as white as bleached bones, and he wondered if she felt sick.

"What is the matter? Are you not well?"

Victoria pointed. "Look, Otto, over there on the branch of that bush. It can't be!" Victoria walked over to an outcropping of brush. There entwined around a scraggly branch, draped a length of violet-colored satin ribbon. The ribbon had been torn in several places, but its color was still rich and vibrant. Carefully, with tender hands, Victoria set free the strip of fabric from its confinement.

Otto watched in silence until at length he said, "Is this like the ribbon you told me about earlier?"

Victoria spoke in a whisper. "No, Otto, this *is* the ribbon."

"But how can you be sure?"

"Well, I suppose I can't be one hundred percent sure, but look here."

Otto watched as Victoria pointed to a small blotch, of what appeared to be black India ink, about four inches from the end of the ribbon. He said, "It looks like a spot of ink in the shape of a heart."

"I remember the day it happened. It was just before my ninth birthday and the winter I took ill. I had started school in the fall and the teacher sat me in front of a disagreeable boy by the name of Michael Clark. He, more often than not, was in trouble with the teacher for something. During our afternoon penmanship lesson, he carelessly flicked his writing pen and sprayed my back with ink. The black splotches stained my hair for a month before they faded away, but Mama never could remove the spot from my pretty ribbon. She asked if I wanted her to trim the ribbon so the mark wouldn't show. I thought about it and told her no. Funny, but I didn't want the ribbon altered, and I thought the little heart-shaped stain was rather sweet."

Victoria looked up from the ribbon and asked, "But, Otto, how did it get here – hundreds of miles away from Springfield?"

Otto shook his head and smiled. "Maybe the wind carried it here. Or maybe someone found it and carried it west only to lose it again. We can never know for sure," Otto reasoned, "but what a story it could tell."

Victoria carefully wound the little strand of ribbon into a roll and carefully placed it inside the leather satchel next to the Amethyst Bottle. "I'll wash it tonight and mend the tears in the satin. With a little tender attention, it will be as good as new."

Otto looked at the girl tightening the rawhide strap to the case at her side. He thought that ribbon was a lot like his friend. With tender attention she had almost become good as new. Victoria lifted her head and smiled at Otto with her eyes. For a second, Otto wondered if she could read his mind when he thought he saw her cheeks flush pink.

He coughed and said, "You seem most happy these days, Victoria, and so very changed from the girl I met in the spring." Otto was pleased that he had thought to loan her the Amethyst Bottle each afternoon. He was certain it had helped her grow stronger.

Victoria opened her mouth to speak, but her face went rigid and her eyes became locked in fear. All she could do was point to the south.

Otto turned around. The scene before him took his breath away. The sky had turned a muddy shade of yellow. Off in the distance a fierce wind seemed to swirl in every direction throwing dust and tumbleweeds into the air. Otto looked at Victoria and asked, "What is it?"

Victoria's mouth had gone dry. She could only choke out one word. "Twister!"

Otto had heard McAuliffe mention to Ghost Walker how lucky the train had been not to run into the swirling mass of winds that could lift a wagon and oxen and toss them into the air like a scrap of paper.

Otto grabbed hold of his friend's hand and shouted over the rising noise from the wind, which seemed to grow louder with each passing second. "Take my hand, Victoria! Whatever happens, do not let go!"

Otto had no idea of the direction of the wagon train. The air was far too hazy. *Try not to panic*, he told himself. Otto pulled Victoria's hand along behind him in an effort to outrun the tornado. He desperately searched for some shelter from the storm.

Otto and Victoria had been struggling against the onslaught of the wind for ten minutes, but they could not escape the fury of the twister which seemed to pick up momentum with each passing second. Pebbles and sand peppered Otto's face. With closed eyes, he frantically gripped tighter the hand of his friend. He turned back to Victoria and blindly yelled, "Don't let go, whatever happens."

Suddenly, a gust of wind thrust a branch into the side of his forehead. The force of the object caused a gash to split the skin open just above his right ear. Blood spurted from the wound as Otto faltered and tumbled to the ground. The action caused Otto's hand to lose its grip with Victoria. In a daze, Otto heard his name swirling with the wind.

"Otto!" Victoria screamed – over and over.

Otto pushed himself up to his hands and knees and blindly crawled in what he hoped was the direction of her ever-fading voice. He forced himself to his feet only to have a large bush ricochet off his face causing thorny branches to slice into his cheeks.

In frantic desperation Otto screamed, "Victoria!" But his voice seemed to be swallowed by the whooshing sound that swirled around his head. The last thing he remembered, as he was lifted into the air, was the strange thought that he was being crushed by a steam engine.

Chapter 9 ~ June 1854 - Indian Territory

A small party of Crow Indians had taken shelter from the mighty winds of Mother Earth in a small ravine. The gulch was protected by a low grassy hill. Time and nature had gathered the earth into a small hill thanks to the prevailing westerly winds which had pushed the soil and sand up against the north-eastern edge of the rift. Seeds and rain had married, and the grasses they formed held the mound together until it had stabilized and become a solid pile of earth. Bison grazed on the tender grasses that grew on the slopes of the hill each spring. Coyotes and mountain lions rested at its peak and used the hill as a vantage point to stalk their prey. Rabbits and prairie dogs burrowed holes in the soil to make homes for their young. Wild flowers decorated the hill with color after a spring rain. The band of Crows had been happy to shelter behind the hill as protection from the encroaching storm.

The five Indian braves forced their ponies to the ground and lay next to their steeds whispering soft words of comfort into their ears to calm the animals. The buffalo hides they had thrown over their bodies helped protect them and their horses from the pounding sand and vegetation. The men knew there was nothing more to do but hope that Mother Earth would not take them to join their ancestors in the next world.

The leader of the little band of Crow was named Black Wolf. He might have been handsome were it not for the pockmarks on his face. The blemishes were a constant reminder of how much he hated white people. He remembered well the white fur trader with many long whiskers on his face. The greasy man, who smelled like a pile of manure, had wandered into the Crow's winter camp when Black Wolf was a young boy of ten. His people had been mistrustful at first, but the man they came to call *Rotting Dog* told them in sign language that he had come to trade pretty red blankets and bright-colored beads for beaver pelts. The elders of Black Wolf's tribe sat in council and decided that the trade would be a good one.

When the fever broke out, his people were baffled. The strange infection caused over half of Black Wolf's tribe to fall ill with a strange disease that caused a high fever and a rash to form on the body. Many of the Crow people died that winter from the sickness of the itchy sores that left scars to those who lived. The chief ordered his people to burn and bury all the red blankets and beads along with the dead. The winter camp, which became known to the Crow as the *Fever of Death*, was abandoned forever.

Black Wolf was one of the lucky ones who lived, but he was forever scarred from the sores of the pox. Years later, Black Wolf would run into *Rotting Dog* as the trapper was skinning a beaver he had just caught in a nearby stream. The stink from his body was exactly as Black Wolf had remembered as a child. The trapper took one look at the Indian's face and knew that he was a goner. Black Wolf shot an arrow straight into the heart of the man before he could even level his knife at the Indian. Black Wolf spat in the earth then walked away without touching the foul smelling mountain man or his gear. He left the trapper's two mules grazing near the stream.

Because he was the leader of the hunting party, Black Wolf knew that it was his responsibility to bring honor to his tribe and capture many ponies from his enemy, the Sioux, and from the stupid white men and women who traversed the land of his forefathers – slaughtering their buffalo and destroying the prairie grass with their ugly wagons. He was proud that his people were known as the greatest horse thieves of the prairie.

As a young child, Black Wolf loved to hear the stories his grandfather told – like the time when he and other brave warriors slithered like snakes into the camp of a group of white men who had, only the day before, introduced themselves as the Lewis and Clark Expedition. The unsuspecting white men slept like babies – only to wake up at sunrise to find that half of their horses had mysteriously disappeared with the morning stars.

Black Wolf pulled the buffalo hide tighter against his head. He wondered how the two women and two braves were faring back at their base camp. The camp was a half-day's ride to the north and hopefully out of danger from the path of the storm. He wistfully thought about the Sioux woman his people called Snow Flower, and wondered if it had been a mistake to bring her with the hunting party. The girl had been with his people for four summers and had surprised Black Wolf by asking him if she could come along with the braves. She told Black Wolf that she could be an asset to the hunting party by acting as an interpreter to any Sioux enemy they might capture along the way. As usual, Black Wolf found it hard to say no to Snow Flower. He was fond of her shiny black hair, smooth skin, and the delicate features of her face.

If Black Wolf were not so arrogant, he would know that Snow Flower would never succumb to the brave's charm. Her heart lay elsewhere. He thought of the many times she had treated him as though he were nothing more than a pesky flea. Black Wolf thought of the times he had considered forcing her to pay more attention to him, but he knew that the girl was the favorite pet of Crooked Knee, the chief of his tribe. *When I have stolen many horses and have captured countless Sioux slaves on this hunt, I will ask the old man if I might take Snow Flower as my wife. The old chief will be so happy with the gifts that I bring before him; he will feel bound to honor my request. Then the snow princess will see who is in charge.* Black Wolf grumbled with annoyance as he recalled the many cold looks given to him by Snow Flower over the years before shifting his thoughts to other matters.

Otto Stanoff dreamed he saw his mother standing in the snow. She was waving a violet ribbon which danced in the icy winds that swirled around her head. He could hear her voice frantically calling his name. Otto called out to her. And, although she could hear his voice, she did not seem to be able to see him. Otto ran to his mother, but the snow was deep and his body was sore. Try as he might, he could not seem to get closer to her. His body was tired and, with each step, his legs sank further and further into the snow. In the end, Otto faltered and tumbled forward sinking into the downy flakes which felt like a cool blanket on his body. "Mama," he called. But it was no use – his voice was as weak as his body. Otto wanted to get up, but his head pounded and he was so very sore. It felt like he had been run over by a herd of buffalo.

Otto opened his eyes. An Indian, with pockmarks on his face, stood over him and leveled a kicking blow into his side. The Indian possessed fierce looking eyes. His hair, although long in the back, had been cropped short on the top and it stood straight up like it had been treated with some type of grease. The Indian screamed at Otto as he lifted his face to the sky and howled like a coyote. Otto's head throbbed. He was thirsty and he felt as though he might throw up. Otto shifted his head to shield his eyes from the sun which was at its peak in the sky.

The air was still and calm and Otto questioned if being lifted into the sky by a twister had only been a dream. He pushed aside the throbbing pain in his head and forced himself to think clearly. He wondered if Victoria was somewhere nearby and tried to sit up. The movement brought pain to every part of his body, and he let out a grown.

The Indian stopped howling and called over to someone in a language that Otto did not understand. In an instant, two Indians trotted over, and stood near Otto. They listened intently to the Indian with pockmarks as he barked out orders. The Indians nodded, bent down, and lifted Otto off the ground. Otto writhed in pain. Every part of his body ached. Yet, despite the pain, it seemed that nothing appeared to be broken. They carried him a few paces away and threw him over a pony like he was a saddle blanket. One of the Indians jumped up behind Otto and the band galloped away across the prairie. The jarring motion of the horse made Otto sick, and he vomited down the side of the horse just before he blacked out.

When Otto woke up, he could hear the sound of voices nearby. He tried moving and realized that one of his legs was tethered to a stake. Otto tried loosening the stake by moving his foot, but it appeared to be embedded deep into the ground. He looked down at his feet and noticed that his shoes and socks were gone, but the rest of his clothes seemed in tact. In the distance, he could hear men laughing and talking in voices too loud. He smelled smoke from a campfire and meat cooking over an open flame. The smell of food reminded his stomach that it was empty. Otto tried to moisten his lips with his tongue, but his tongue was swollen and his lips felt dry and cracked.

Slowly, he opened his eyes just enough so he could survey the area and not let anyone know he had regained consciousness.

Two women, one older and one younger, talked softly as they tended the meat they were roasting on a spit. Otto looked closer and inwardly groaned. The older woman, who possessed a generous belly, appeared to be wearing his shoes. He counted seven, or was it eight, Indians resting on buffalo hides talking in animated conversation? *Too many for me to gain the upper hand*, Otto thought. He was surprised to see the sun setting on the horizon and he wondered where the day had gone. Otto felt his heart sinking with the sun in the distance, as he also wondered where Victoria had gone. He hoped she had made it to safety during the storm, although he knew her chances must have been slim. He was glad that she had been wearing the Amethyst Bottle at her side and hoped that it would help her find her way back to the wagon train and her folks.

The younger woman looked over in his direction and Otto quickly closed his eyes pretending to be asleep. But Otto realized that he was shaking from the cool night air or perhaps from the shock of the bruises to his body. He listened to her steps as she walked over to where the men sat and spoke with a voice that sounded gentle to his ears. When the man barked an answer back to her, Otto thought he remembered the voice as the Indian who had kicked him in the side.

Otto shuddered, but this time it was not just from the cold. The boy knew he had been in some tough situations living on the streets of Five Points, but something in the pockmarked Indian's eyes had told him that he was in real trouble. Otto listened to the soft padding of feet make their way to where he lay. The girl said something to him that he did not understand, but something in her voice calmed him and he opened his eyes.

Otto looked up into the face of the prettiest Indian girl he had ever seen in his life. The fading light from the sun cast its glow on her face. She had large expressive brown eyes and a small straight nose that set off the creamy brown color of her face. The girl took Otto by the back of his neck and gently lifted his head so she could place a soft leather container filled with water to his lips. Otto drank from the container, and thought that the water tasted sweeter than anything he had ever put in his mouth. Otto figured the girl looked to be about eighteen. Her hair was parted in the middle and she had fashioned it into two simple braids. She wore no adornments in her hair except for one small white feather attached toward the bottom of the left braid.

This angel of kindness allowed Otto to drink from the flask for only a few seconds before she took it away from his lips. Otto was very thirsty. He was about to change his opinion of the girl when she lifted the pouch and offered the water to him again. The gentle girl repeated the process until Otto came to understand that she wanted him to drink the water slowly. The young woman was patient, and let him come back to the water until he signaled that he had taken his fill. She washed the gash on the side of his head with water. He tried to thank her, but she put her hand to her lips as a signal that Otto should not speak. She gave a furtive glance over to where the men sat talking then looked back at Otto. She spoke not a word, but something in her eyes told him that he should be very careful. He nodded his head and the girl gracefully rose up from the ground and traced her steps back to the campfire.

Otto pretended to sleep. He listened as the Indians ate their meal with the men continuing to talk in lively voices. Otto wondered, if perhaps, they too were happy to have escaped the fury of the cyclone and needed to tell the others of their good fortune. He was very hungry, but no food was offered to him. Soon after it got dark, Otto could hear the sounds of people preparing for sleep. The night was mild and Otto was grateful that he had worn a sweater over his flannel shirt when he had left camp that fateful morning. At least he knew he would not suffer from the chilly night-air. He thought of his mother and the strange dream of her waving the violet ribbon in the snowstorm. He wondered if the wagon train had suffered from the ravages of the storm. Then Otto prayed that Victoria was safe from all harm.

The hours of darkness passed slowly for Otto. In time, he heard the familiar sounds of slumber from the Indians as they slept. He opened his eyes no more than a slit and was not surprised to see one of the Indians standing guard near the fire. Slowly, he rolled over on his side so that his back faced toward the camp. With a hand that trembled, Otto slowly reached up and felt for his mother's crest under his clothes. He let out a silent cry in agony. The beloved crest was gone. He wondered if it had been lost in the storm. Silent tears stung his eyes.

Chapter 10 ~ June 1854 - Indian Territory

Otto had been at the camp for three days barely able to move. He reasoned that it must be midweek and with each passing day he knew the wagon train would be moving ever further away from him. The problem was he had no idea in which direction the Indians had taken him when they had thrown him over the horse. Even if Otto could escape, he would not know where to find McAuliffe and Ghost Walker, other than follow the path of the setting sun. Besides, Otto had no shoes. His boots were gone and he wondered if the calluses on his feet, from his days at Five Points, were strong enough to carry him across the rough land. He felt that trekking across the prairie in his bare feet could prove to be a challenge. Still, he was determined that he would try if given the chance to escape.

The young Indian girl, with the small white feather in her hair, seemed to be in charge of nursing him back to health. She tended to his wounds and gave him small bits of food to keep him from starving and a potion mixed with some foul tasting plants. Otto tried to decline the drink, but she insisted that he must take the medicine. Within a day, he had been able to stand and hobble around the tethered stake.

Otto reckoned that the Indians were intending to make him a slave for their tribe and they needed him well so he could work. He had heard stories of the capture of white people who were stolen from their homes – never to be seen again.

On the forth day, Otto was allowed to hobble about the camp, but he had been warned, through the use of hand motions, that he must always stay within eyesight of the camp. His heart sank as he brought a bundle of sticks to the large

Indian woman who cooked the food. When she barked at him and pointed to the ground where he should drop the wood, Otto saw his mother's crest around her neck. Otto pointed to the crest, but she merely looked at him and laughed. Otto was relieved it hadn't been lost in the storm, but knew his chances of getting it back were slim.

Usually, the Indian with the pockmarks on his face led most of the Indians off on their horses during the day, but he always left one or two Indians back at camp to watch Otto and to perhaps protect the women. Otto guessed that they must be looking for buffalo, but one day they came back with five horses. Otto saw that the horses had brands on their hides, so he knew that they must have been stolen from soldiers or some unsuspecting pioneers traveling west.

On that day, Otto's heart leapt with joy. The boy had observed that the hunting party had headed south that morning. He calculated that there must be an overland trail within one day's ride judging from the time the band of Indians had been away from the camp. If he could steal a horse he might find a way to rejoin McAuliffe and the others.

During the time of his confinement, Otto watched the habits of the group carefully – hoping that he might discover a way to outwit his captors. The Indian with pockmarks on his face, who had kicked Otto in the side, was especially hateful to him and Otto secretly assigned the name of *Pockface* to him. Otto thought that Pockface seemed to be very fond of the young Indian girl whom Otto had come to think of as *White Feather*. Otto observed that Pockface often tried to engage White Feather in conversation, or he would motion for her to join him on his buffalo hide as he sat eating the evening meal. Otto also witnessed that White Feather acted guarded around the Indian – almost as though she was afraid of him. When White Feather wanted a favor from Pockface, she would grace him with a smile. But when her back was turned away from him, Otto saw the traces of cheerless frown lines form near her pretty eyes. He wondered if his hope to escape might rest with the unhappy girl. Otto's chance came with a stroke of luck.

Otto sat near the morning campfire gnawing on some rabbit bones the older woman, who cooked most of the meals, had thrown him from leftovers that the group had shared for the morning meal. After Black Wolf and his men had headed out of camp, Snow Flower motioned for Otto to help her fetch water from a nearby stream. The day was sunny, but from the look of the dark clouds on the horizon, a rainstorm seemed to be moving in from the south.

The band of Indians was traveling light and had brought no tipis to shelter them from the encroaching storm. It had rained briefly the day before and Snow Flower and the others had simply crossed their legs and placed a buffalo hide over their heads while they patiently waited for the storm to pass. Otto had been tethered to his stake and was miserable and cold as the soaking rain passed over their camp. He had been amazed when the Indians emerged from their furry shelters dry and hardly the worse for wear.

Otto waded with Snow Flower into the stream until the water was knee-level. Otto looked down into the clear cold water and admired a large brown trout swimming in the distance. The girl motioned for Otto to remain still. He watched, in fascination, as she held her hands inches above the surface of the water. Neither moved a muscle when the trout swam over to where they stood. With lightning speed, Snow Flower plunged her hands into the water and grabbed the slippery fish as though she were plucking an egg from the nest of a chicken.

Otto was excited and more than a little impressed. Without thinking, Otto blurted out, "Wicin nape cetan." Roughly speaking, he had declared that the girl had hands the speed of a hawk in the Lakota language of the Sioux.

With the brown trout still wiggling in her hands, Snow Flower looked at Otto with an odd expression on her face. Otto bit his lip and wished that he had kept his mouth shut. He knew that these people were not Sioux. He inwardly groaned. What if this tribe hated the Sioux? They might hand out harsher treatment to him if they knew he was familiar with the language of an enemy tribe. Otto quickly looked down at the water and wished he could drown the Sioux words at the bottom of the stream. Otto thought, *I'll play dumb. Maybe she will forget the words in the excitement of the moment.*

The girl threw the trout up on the grass where it flopped about and she called out to the other woman in the unfamiliar language. The heavier-set woman came over and picked up the fish. Snow Flower spoke briefly to the woman who happily cradled the fish in her arms like a baby. Otto stood motionless as the older woman waddled back to the campfire. Otto watched the girl turn her attention back to the water. Looking as though she was planning on catching more fish, the girl whispered softly to Otto in the Sioux language, "You speak Lakota?"

Otto played dumb and pretended that he did not understand her words. The girl spoke softly telling him that she was Sioux and that he could trust her that she would not betray him. There was something in the desperate look of her eyes that told Otto that she was telling the truth.

Otto began to speak, but the girl he had come to know as White Feather, grabbed his hand pretending to be excited about finding another fish. During that moment, she placed her finger to her lips and Otto knew that she wanted him to speak softly.

He whispered, "I have learned a few words of the Lakota language from a friend of mine who is Sioux."

"I am Sioux, but have been with the Crow people for many moons. I have been hoping for a way to get back to my people and came on this hunt for that reason. Say nothing and do as I order."

Otto's spirits soared. He had not understood all her words but he recognized that she was Sioux and not like the others. This was just the break he had been praying for. Maybe, through this girl, he could find his way back to the wagon train.

The girl filled two large gourds with water and motioned for Otto to follow her back to the camp. Otto was surprised when she kicked him in the leg and snarled at him to take the water to the other woman who was at work cleaning the trout. Otto did as he was ordered.

He watched out of the corner of his eye as the girl walked over to where an Indian guard was resting near the captured horses and began speaking the unfamiliar words in an animated voice.

"Greetings, Tall Tree, I see that Boiling Pot is cleaning the fish I caught for your meal. I want to take this lazy boy with me to find some more buffalo chips for our fire. I can see that he is feeling better, and I think he should work harder for our people."

Tall Tree looked up at the pretty girl and wished that Black Wolf was not planning on taking her for his wife. He, too, would have liked to make a play for her. As Snow Flower looked down at him with a tender smile on her face, Tall Tree considered her request. "Yes, take the lazy boy to do your work for you, but stay where I can see you, Snow Flower."

The girl thanked Tall Tree and walked over to where Otto was sitting. She kicked him again and harshly motioned for him to follow her. Otto trotted off after the girl as she walked across the prairie.

When the pair was some distance from the camp the girl turned her body away from the watchful eyes of Tall Tree and spoke to Otto in Lakota. "Pick up that buffalo chip and place it in the basket if you understand?" Otto bent down and picked up one dried round of manure and put it into a woven basket. Otto watched, as the girl he had come to know as White Feather, smiled. She and Otto continued to walk with their faces turned away from the camp. "I am Sioux, but was stolen from my home when I was a little girl. For many rains, I have looked for a way to find my people. When I heard that Black Wolf and the others were coming south on this hunting party, I prayed to my ancestors that he would bring me along too. I plan to go away from here tonight. If you understand pick up three chips." When Otto did as she asked, the girl closed her eyes and let out a sigh.

"Black Wolf and the others will be gone for two days. Last night he told Boiling Pot and me that he had spotted a herd of buffalo a half day's ride to the east. The men came back to camp last night to prepare for the hunt. That is why he rode out with all the men at sunrise leaving only Tall Tree to guard the camp. It will take Black Wolf and the other braves two days to hunt down and bring back the meat. This may be our only chance. Do you understand my words?" Otto bent over and nodded his head.

"Leave the plan of escape to me, and whatever you do, do not eat the food at sunset. If you understand, pick up two more chips." Otto picked up two more chips, heaved a sigh of relief, and smiled.

Otto watched nervously from his place tethered to the stake. Boiling Pot hummed as she made a stew from dried buffalo meat and a vegetable that looked like a potato but was actually a root which anchored certain tall grasses that grew along the shallow bank of the stream. Otto was not overly fond of the root's slightly bitter taste, but he ate it willingly. The root helped fill the empty feeling that was always present in his stomach. Otto looked at the sky to the south. The storm, which Otto had noticed earlier in the day, was slow moving, but Otto felt certain it would find its way to their camp sometime during the night. Otto wondered what words were being spoken as the three Indians exchanged, what appeared to be, pleasant conversation around the campfire.

"You were smart to hobble the horses together, Tall Tree. It looks as though Mother Earth will bring much water from the sky with the rising of the moon." Snow Flower looked at the Indian sitting on his buffalo hide near the warmth of the campfire and smiled shyly. Tall Tree gazed over at Snow Flower and thought the girl looked especially pretty when she smiled.

"Yes, Snow Flower. It is as you say." Tall Tree flashed a huge smile back at Snow Flower showing her a mouth filled with crooked teeth. Thinking that he may have a chance to win her favor after all, Tall Tree said, "I see that you have tied the boy's leg to the stake. Do you not wish to feed him tonight?"

Snow Flower pretended to be annoyed. "The boy needs to be taught a lesson. He is lazy and did not pick up as many buffalo chips as he should have. I think he needs to spend a night without food."

"You make a good point, Snow Flower."

"If he goes to sleep with an empty belly and is pelted with rain from Mother Earth tonight, I think he will be humbled and will make a better effort to work harder when the sun rises in the morning."

Boiling Pot stirred the soup and laughed. "Let the boy go hungry! That will leave more food for the three of us to share. I hope Black Wolf is victorious with the hunt for buffalo. My mouth is watering for fresh meat."

Snow Flower cleared her voice and spoke casually. "Boiling Pot, I have some lovely herbs that I have been saving for a special occasion. The herbs are rare and hard to find. With your consent, I would like to use some tonight to flavor the food. I know that you are famous among our people for the special way you blend the dried leaves to make the food so tasty. I am just a silly young girl and would not have my feelings hurt if you wish to refuse my gift."

Boiling Pot did not answer the girl right away. She was somewhat fussy about the meals she served the men and was not sure she wanted her special recipe tampered with.

Snow Flower turned her head casually away from Boiling Pot and looked like she too was about to change her mind. She began to close the little leather pouch holding the dried leaves when she uttered innocently, "I once used the leaves to season the meat for our chief, Crooked Knee. He said the flavor was uncommonly agreeable. He flattered me by adding that it was the most delicious flavor he had ever tasted. I am sure that he was only being kind to a young girl."

Boiling Pot's head shot up from its position leaning over the pot of stew. She looked at the young girl casually closing the small leather pouch that held the special herbs. "In truth, Snow Flower, I have grown somewhat tired of the same old way that I mix the herbs for the stew. Something different might be just what I need to enhance flavors in the pot. Where did you find this special plant and why do I not know about it?"

"The plant is very hard to find, but I found the unusual bush on our march to the summer camp last spring. The plant was a favorite that my mother used to flavor her meat when I was a little girl. I had almost forgotten that it existed. "

At that moment, Boiling Pot was once again reminded that Snow Flower had been taken from her own people, the Sioux, during one of the Crow's many raids. The girl had been with her people for so many summers that it had escaped her memory. She also knew that Snow Flower was a favorite of their chief, Crooked Knee.

Boiling Pot thought back to the summer when the young girl had been brought to the Crow encampment. Back then, the girl did not speak the beautiful language of the Crow. The young girl had only been with the tribe for a week when some of the older women had decided to have some fun with her. Boiling Pot had watched from her place at the campfire as some of the women were kicking the child in the backside and pushing her around while others stood by and laughed at the girl's discomfort. The women were so occupied with their fun that they did not see their chief, Crooked Knee, ride into the camp on his black and white pony. The wise chief noticed the disturbance and rode closer to the women. He watched from his horse as the young girl stood bravely in the circle of hecklers and took the abuses of the older women with courage. One of the younger women, named Dark Sky, shoved the girl hard and she fell onto the dirt. Crooked Knee knew that the child must be very scared, but he watched as she shed not a tear. The chief threw his leg over the neck of his pony and slipped off his horse. He walked over to the circle of women with a sour expression on his face. The women stopped and looked sheepishly at their leader when they realized that he had taken time from his busy day to become interested in what they were doing.

The beloved chief spoke in a gentle yet commanding voice. "Why do you torment this young girl so? You treat her with no more respect than you might have for a lazy dog. Tell me, is the girl not doing what you have asked her to do so that she might earn the right to eat at our campfire?"

One of the women named Squawking Duck took it upon herself to speak for the group. "No, Crooked Knee, the girl is a good worker." She looked at the young girl crouched in the dirt and felt somewhat ashamed. "We were just having some fun with the young girl because she does not speak the beautiful words of the Crow."

The chief frowned at the circle of women. "This young girl must be very sad to have been taken from the only people she has ever known, yet look how brave she is at the hands of you silly women. She does what you ask, yet you abuse her for your own amusement like a foolish child might do to a puppy."

Crooked Knee held out his hand and helped pull the girl to her feet. The girl's grip was firm and the chief became taken, not only with her beauty, but her incredible bravery. The wise chief looked into the eyes of the girl. He noticed that the eyes held no fear in them, only a very great sadness. At that instant, his heart went out to her.

"I will name this girl Snow Flower. She is like the hardy red flower that pushes its way through the snow to brighten and give color to the mountains of our winter camp. Know this. Treat the girl well for she will be like a daughter to me. Teach her the beautiful language of the Crow and show her the ways of our people."

Boiling Pot looked across the campfire and smiled at Snow Flower. She said, "Season the stew with your leaves. If the flavor of your plant is agreeable to my tongue, we will find this bush and I will add the leaf to my collection."

Snow Flower smiled. She opened the small leather amulet containing the dried leaves and added half of the contents to the pot of stew. She hoped that her hand did not shake because her stomach felt like the tornado that had just passed across the prairie a few days earlier.

Otto only pretended to sleep. He watched the scene around the campfire unfold like a Russian dance. The girl he called White Feather kept a lively flow of animated conversation going throughout the meal as Tall Tree and the other woman ate their dinner. The fire, which cast its glow on the group as they shared their evening meal, seemed to mirror the warmth of easy exchange among the three. Two of the people in the group did not seem to notice that the youngest member encircling the fire only picked at the dried buffalo stew.

At first Otto was cautious, but as the evening meal progressed, it seemed that the three Indians had forgotten that he was even alive. From time to time, Otto noticed the splintering of lightening illuminate the sky to the south. The light cast an eerie glow on the desolate prairie, but the encroaching storm seemed to do nothing to dampen the spirits of the little group.

When the meal had ended, Otto saw White Feather excuse herself and walk into the dark. Otto assumed she was seeking privacy to relieve herself. Otto was surprised when the girl slipped behind a bush where the others could not see her. Out of the corner of his eye, Otto saw the girl stick her hand into her mouth and quietly vomit what little soup she had eaten for dinner. The gesture suddenly reminded Otto of the brightly dressed pack of Indians who had followed the train some time back, and the way they would throw up the rancid food they had found by the sides of the trail. The memory of that time shocked Otto as it seemed so very long ago. He pushed away the thought and focused on what might be his only chance to get back to his people.

Otto muffled a chuckle as he watched the older woman try to stoke up the fire. Otto noticed that as she bent over to pick from a pile of buffalo chips, she almost fell forward with her unsteady gait. The woman reminded Otto of a drunk he had once known in Five Points named Irish. Otto found that the male Indian was trying desperately to stay awake on his buffalo hide, but his hand kept slipping off his head as his elbow spayed out flat on the hide. Otto watched the young Indian girl walk down to the stream and rinse her mouth out with water.

By the time Snow Flower returned to the light of the fire, both Indians were resting on their hides trying to stay awake. The young girl said nothing. Instead, she casually removed the pot from the fire and tipped its remaining contents into the dirt. The girl removed three water skins from a stake near the fire and announced that she was going to fill them with water. The only sound she heard in return was the crackling of the fire.

Snow Flower laced her way to the stream feeling slightly unsteady on her feet. Her head felt like it had been stuffed with the fluffy white pods that were carried with the wind from the giant cottonwood trees each spring. She dropped to her knees and topped off the leather skins with water. Snow Flower then decided to dunk her entire head into the stream. The action helped clear her head from the potent plant that could make a person sleep for an entire day.

Snow Flower knew that if Boiling Pot would have paid more attention, she might have noticed that the plant was not an herb for cooking, but a plant known to her people as *tolache*, which was a powerful medicine. The shaman of her tribe had once used the jimsonweed on her brother so that the boy would lie still so he could set his broken leg. He had given small amounts of the plant to Snow Flower's mother to help ease the boy's pain over the next few days. It was true when she had told Boiling Pot that she had found the plant on the way to the summer camp. She had stored it in the small leather bag she wore around her neck. She had been waiting for a time it might prove useful in making her escape.

Snow Flower made her way to Otto feeling a little clearer in the head since dunking it in the stream. She pulled a knife from inside her moccasin boots and quickly cut the cord that tethered him to the stake. "Come. We will take the horses with us."

"My shoes," whispered Otto pointing to his feet.

Snow Flower shook her head. "No. It is too dangerous to try and remove the shoes from her feet."

Otto stood his ground and pointed to his chest and over to where Boiling Pot lay passed out by the campfire. Otto saw that White Feather wanted to say no, but something in the boy's eyes softened her heart. Together, they crept over to the snoring woman. Otto knelt at her side and watched as White Feather was preparing to cut the rawhide strap from the woman's neck with her knife.

All of a sudden, Boiling Pot opened her eyes, lifted her head, and grabbed Otto's arm. The strength of her grip caused Otto to freeze with fear. She mumbled a few slurred words at Otto. Then, just as quickly, the woman crumpled back onto the hide. But not before Snow Flower, with the speed of a bobcat, snatched the cord from Boiling Pot's neck and handed it to Otto. Otto secured the leather strip around his neck and tucked the crest under his sweater.

Otto was sad about the shoes, but he knew that it would be foolish to further endanger their chances of slipping away from the camp. He followed the girl to where the horses were hobbled. Otto noticed White Feather speaking softly to the horses to calm them. One at a time, and with a patience that made Otto a little nervous, she removed the horses from their snares. Using the same rope, Otto helped the girl fashion the ropes into halters. When all of the horses had been made ready, she put her hand to her lips and motioned for Otto to follow her away from the camp.

Otto and the Indian girl walked across the prairie with the trailing horses until the light from the campfire was a mere speck on the horizon. A flash of lightening crackled in the distance and several of the horses reared up in panic.

White Feather looked at Otto and asked, "Can you ride?"

"Yes."

"Good. We will take two of the soldiers' horses and untie the others. Hopefully Mother Earth will help scatter them across the land in many different directions. It will make it harder for Black Wolf and the others to track us. The rain will also cover our tracks. Do you understand?"

Otto had not comprehended all of the girl's words, but he caught just enough to understand the general plan. Otto carefully considered the five army horses that Black Wolf had brought into the camp a few days ago and chose two sturdy Quarter Horses for them to ride. He walked the horses away from the others and held onto their reins tightly as he watched the girl carefully remove the halters of the remaining ponies. One by one, she slapped the horses on their backsides and urged them on with words of encouragement to help scatter them in various directions.

Otto and White Feather mounted the two army horses and coaxed them south in the direction of the oncoming storm.

Chapter 11 ~ June 1854 - Mormon Trail

"I do not think it would be wise to go to this camp," the Indian girl whispered nervously to Otto in Lakota.

Otto looked over and could see from the expression on the girl's face that she was afraid to enter the settlers' encampment. But Otto's stomach ached with hunger and a gut-feeling told him that they might not get another chance for help. "Let us watch first before we say yes or no to these people," he answered. Otto silently thanked Ghost Walker for teaching him the beautiful language of the Sioux.

Otto adjusted his position on his belly and looked down onto the camp from a small hill that rose up about twenty feet off the surface of the flat prairie. He looked back down the other side of the edge to check on their two horses. The tired animals were munching on some tender shoots of grass, which grew near a watering hole that looked to have increased in size from the overnight storm. Otto glanced across at White Feather who was lying beside him, then down at the small group of pioneers who were just beginning to rise from their tents in harmony with the sun mounting its charge on the eastern horizon. The boy sighed wistfully. The scene unfolding before him, reminded him of his time with McAuliffe and Ghost Walker on the wagon train. In one respect, that life seemed so long ago. And yet, he guessed that it had been only five days since he had walked into the belly of a tornado with Victoria. He wondered if he would ever see them again. Victoria's face popped into his mind's eye and he realized how much he missed his friend. He again prayed that she had somehow survived the fury of the twister and was found safe and unharmed.

Otto and the Indian girl watched the systematic sequence of events developing below them. One woman stoked up the campfire until a nice little blaze erupted. The woman then greased a large cast iron pan which she placed on an iron cooking grate next to a large pot of what looked to be beans. Another woman reached into a wooden barrel marked, *flour*, and spooned a sizable portion of the powdery wheat into a large tin bowl and efficiently began to incorporate the flour with lard, salt and water. Neither of the women spoke, and yet they worked quickly and in unison to make the biscuits as though they were performing a play they had rehearsed together a thousand times. Everyone in the group appeared to have a job to do in breaking down the tents and loading the handcarts for the day's march west. Even the children worked diligently – attending to small tasks like dressing the younger children and filling canteens from the river.

The wagon train was small in size and seemed poorly outfitted to Otto. The group had only one covered wagon with four bedraggled oxen, two pack mules, and six or seven handcarts, which the men and women were packing with their canvas tents and blankets. Otto counted out six men, nine women and more than a dozen children in varying stages of growth. The setting looked harmless enough to Otto's mind – just another group of pioneers heading west on the overland trail. Yet, still he waited.

Otto and White Feather had ridden the army horses hard throughout the night. At times, the rain had beat upon them so severe, the going had been slow. The two worried that the horses might slip and come up lame, so for part of the night they had walked the steeds across the rough terrain. As miserable as the night had been, the heavy rain became a blessing. The tremendous runoff from the downpour washed away the horses' hoof prints. Sometimes, Otto wondered if they had been going in circles, but White Feather, seemed to have an uncanny sense of direction. Even without the stars to guide them, she appeared to know the terrain. She took the lead and assured Otto that they were heading south. Otto was happy to hang back and let her guide them away from their captors. The two spoke little and kept moving until at last, they had come to their place on the hill.

While resting from their look-out, the two finally had gotten the chance to talk in whispers. The Indian girl told Otto that she felt certain that their trail would be hard to track, even for an experienced group of Crow. Otto smiled when he envisioned the self-important Indian he had secretly nicknamed, Pockface, riding into camp to discover that his stolen horses, his white captive, and the Indian girl he was so very fond of were gone. He thought of the heavy-set Indian woman who now possessed his only pair of shoes, and the lanky Indian brave with crooked teeth. Otto knew that the pair would be blamed for bringing such terrible shame upon the Indian brave's honor. Otto cared little for the humiliation that would tarnish the brave's standing among his people. He only cared that they would get as far away from the angry Crow as time and distance would carry them.

Otto shifted his position in the grass onto his side and looked down at his bare feet. What he saw made him frown. Scratches, cuts, and a deeply gashed toe that he had stubbed on a rock, were mingled with blood and mud. He grieved for the boots given to him as a gift from Doc Simpson, but was again immensely grateful that his mother's crest had returned to him. Otto noticed that his pants were dirty and torn in several places. He turned back on his stomach, looked across at White Feather, and wrinkled his brow. The girl looked hardly the worse for wear. The crisp little white feather was still neatly attached to her left braid, and her soft buckskin dress had not a muddy mark on it. Otto thought of Ghost Walker and the dignity of his manner and thought, *There is such an poised grace in the way these people carry themselves.*

Otto was pulled from his thoughts when the sound of the biscuit-ladies' voices called out in unison to bring the others to breakfast. The small party of travelers quickly gathered around the campfire for the simple meal. Otto watched as the entire group joined hands and bowed their heads in what looked to be a prayer. He looked over at the Indian girl and smiled.

Searching for the correct words in Lakota, Otto said, "These are good people. Do not fear. They will help us on our journey. Come with me." Otto reached out to her.

The girl looked worried, and for a moment Otto thought she would not take his hand, but he breathed a sigh of relief when she timidly nodded her head.

Micah Dunne looked up from his place around the campfire and scowled. "Look, Pa, there's a white boy and an Injun gal a-comin' over the rise with two horses."

Bishop Dennis Dunne looked in the direction of the intruders and calmly spoke to his son in a soft voice. "Ya best git my riffle off the wagon, Micah."

The fifteen-year-old boy ran over to the covered wagon and retrieved the Winchester rifle from its place on the floor under the seat. The rest of the unit had already gathered into a tight cluster – with older children holding younger ones and mothers cradling the youngest babies in their arms. Micah handed the rifle to his father and then proceeded to count the members. When he was satisfied that no one was missing, he shouted, "All here, Pa." The boy quickly took up a place in line behind the wake of the older men.

To Otto, the little group, who had gathered behind the wall of men armed with guns, axes, and clubs, looked ready and alert, as though they had practiced this course of action many times before. Otto stopped twenty feet from the camp. He handed the horse's rein to White Feather and raised both of his hands in the air. "Please," he declared, "we wish to bring you no harm. We are lost and are looking to catch up with our wagon train and its leader, Cornelius P. McAuliffe. Do you know this man?"

"Nope. Never heard of him," answered Dennis.

"May we approach?"

"Not just yet," Dunne commanded. "Watcha doing travelin' with an Injun gal?"

Otto stood his ground and said, "About five days back, I was captured by a band of Crow Indians. They took me north about one day's ride from here. This Indian girl was a captive as well. She helped me run away so that I might get back to my wagon train and she might find her people."

Bishop Dunne was a man who rarely got ruffled. He could see that the boy and girl were traveling with a few leather containers that looked to hold water and a pair of bareback horses. Still, as leader of the small group of Latter Day Saints heading to join other Mormons in Salt Lake City, he did not want any more trouble than he already had as the person in charge. In particular, he did not want to anger a pack of Indians who might be riding into his camp looking for revenge.

"Where'd ya git them army horses?"

Otto looked square into the leader's steely gray eyes. The man was tall, and built like a black bear Otto had once seen in Russia. His hands were enormous and looked as though they might easily crush the rifle he held in his hands. He had a coal-black beard and a crop of thick black hair that stuck out in every direction. There was something very imposing about his bearing, and Otto knew it would be important to make a good first-impression.

Otto cleared his throat and declared, "The horses were among a group that had been brought into the Indian camp a few days back while I was a prisoner. I see that they are stolen. When we escaped, we let the others run free and we take these to help make our…how do you say… run…no, escape."

The younger man blurted out, "You must be lying, boy! How could a backwoods emigrant like yourself and an Indian girl outfox an entire band of Indians? There's no way…."

Otto watched as the impressive man with the rifle turned his head to the side and cut the young boy's words off with a stern look. Then he calmly preached, "Micah, the Good Book says, *judge not, lest ye be judged.*" Otto could see Micah's face flush red.

The bishop turned his attention back to Otto and added, "Well, you may as well go on, stranger, and answer the question of my impetuous boy."

Otto sucked in his breath and replied, "Yesterday, most of the men go on a two-day hunt for buffalo. They leave me guarded by only one brave, and one other woman whose job is to cook for the men. It was by luck that I came to know that this Indian girl was being held against her will like me. Last night, she put some powerful medicine in the food of the two who watched over us. While they slept, we took two of the horses and rode south until we found your camp. This is truth and I will swear to it on my father's grave."

Bishop Dunne looked at the boy with dirty clothes and no shoes. He felt that his story rang true, but still he did not want any trouble so he asked, "When are these Indians expected back to the camp?"

"They most likely will come back sometime tomorrow. I reckon it will take them a while to organize the search for us, if it is what they choose to do, and another day or so to catch up with us. Please, if we might trouble you for a bite of food, we will travel on once we have rested."

Dunne looked at Otto through tired eyes and said, "Wait right where you are for a moment." The bishop turned around to face the members of the little group and Otto could hear them talking in soft voices. In time, the leader turned back to Otto and said, "If what you say is true, and I have a feeling it is, it seems reasonable that you're not in danger today. My name is Bishop Dunne. This is my wife Rose, and my other wife Martha. You've already gotten acquainted with my son, Micah. I'll introduce ya to the rest of the group just shortly. Come and join us for breakfast. I s'pose it'd be alright to spend the day resting up in our covered wagon as we move west. I imagine you're worn out from travelin' all night in that hideous storm. I know it disturbed my sleep. Come nighttime you can head out on your own."

Otto listened to the kind words of the bishop and felt very grateful. It was clear to him that these people were in a struggle to make it across the wilderness to this place called Salt Lake. What great fortune had guided him and White Feather into this camp – where the people were willing to share what little supplies they possessed!

Dennis turned to Micah and added, "Son, take the horses for grazin', then tie 'em to the wagon after breakfast." He then looked at one of the wives whom Otto had observed preparing the biscuits and added, "Mother Rose, get these strangers some biscuits and beans."

Otto breathed easier when the boy named Micah made no more protests, but quickly did as he was asked. He turned to White Feather who had been as silent and still as a post and said in Lakota, "Do not fear. These people will help us."

White Feather nodded her head and followed Otto over to the fire.

The covered wagon was packed with supplies, but Otto and White Feather wedged themselves in between some sacks of grain and quickly drifted off to sleep. Otto did not dream and became agitated when he was unexpectedly pulled from his deep slumber by a gentle tapping on his shoulder.

Otto's heart skipped a pace and he quickly sat up. Immediately, he noticed that the wagon had stopped moving. The Indian girl motioned that she wanted to go outside. Otto thought that maybe she wanted to commune with nature. He nodded his head as he pushed the drowsy feeling from his brain and wondered how long they had been asleep. Otto crawled to the back of the wagon and lifted the flap. He saw that the sun was directly overhead, and the band of travelers had stopped for what appeared to be the noon meal. Otto climbed down from the wagon and was instantly greeted by two young girls who looked to be about his age. As White Feather drifted off down to the river by herself, Otto was escorted by the giggling girls over the main group of adults who were finishing up another meal of biscuits and beans around a small campfire. A few men were napping while some of the children ran happily around the camp playing some form of tag.

Bishop Dunne stood up and motioned for Otto to join the circle of people. "You've been sleeping for about six hours. Ya must've been powerful-tired to be able to sleep with all that jarring motion of the wagon. I mean to tighten the axel on the wheels when we reach Fort Laramie."

Otto perked up, "Are we close to Fort Laramie? For that is where Captain McAuliffe is heading. He wishes to rest there for a few days before leaving the prairie and heading over the Rocky Mountains and then over the Sierras and into California."

"According to my notes, Fort Laramie is about a week's ride up ahead – maybe three to four days for you being unencumbered with wagons and all. If you got separated from your group five day's ago, they should almost be there by now. Perhaps you can catch them there. Or, perhaps ya might want to try your luck in Salt Lake. We're looking for young able men to help build our city."

The two girls who had escorted Otto over to the fire began giggling again and Otto nervously shifted his seat.

"Hush now! Never mind these foolish girls, Otto. They're just 'bout gettin' at an age where they're on a hunt for a husband. Help yourself to some grub and tell us a little about yourself."

Otto noticed that the bishop's son, Micah, seemed agitated with the attention he had been getting from the girls. The Mormon boy scowled as he whittled on a stick with a sharp knife. Otto thought, *What is this to go on a **hunt** for a husband?* He made a mental note to ask Captain McAuliffe about this strange custom. Otto swallowed hard and cleared his throat. He was at a loss for words. The giggling girls looked to be about the same age as Victoria. Otto thought of his friend and inwardly blushed. He just couldn't think of her as being old enough to go on some ritual *hunt* in order to get married. Otto shifted uncomfortably in his seat. He looked back in the direction of the river, but White Feather was nowhere to be seen. He hoped she was okay.

Otto turned his attention back to the kind people seated around the fire and finally found the calmness to speak. He decided to change the subject. "I know this word *grub*. A man named Biscuit who works for Captain McAuliffe on our wagon train calls us to eat his grub." Otto reached out for a tin plate handed to him by the wife named Martha. "Thank you for the *grub*, Ma'am."

Martha smiled and declared earnestly, "You best eat up. After you've had yer fill, I'll tend to the gash on yer toe."

"That would be most kind." Otto turned to Bishop Dunne and asked, "Are we on the overland trail?"

"The overland trail is on the other side of the river. Most Mormons like to travel on the north side of the Platte so as to not be bothered by folks. Where ya from, Otto?"

Otto looked across at Bishop Dunne and said, "My full name is Otto Stanoff, and I am a Jewish boy from Russia. I have been in America for one year and six months. I have been on wagon train since April traveling west to find my brother, Ivan, who is in San Francisco. I have not seen him for many years.

"You're a Jew! Well, thump a drum and sound the horn! We have some things in common, Otto."

Otto looked up and let out a sign of relief when he saw White Feather standing next to him. He was always a little unnerved with the way the girl would appear at his side having never heard her footsteps. White Feather had washed her face and hands and looked as clean as the inside of Biscuit's kettle. Otto glanced down at his own hands and wished he had thought to spruce up a might before coming over to the fire. He knew Mama would have scolded him for his terrible manners.

Otto motioned for White Feather to sit next to him. He watched as she gracefully crossed her legs and seemed to float to the ground. The woman named Rose was already in the process of handing over another plate of food. Otto noticed that the Indian girl smiled shyly as she gathered the plate of grub into her hands.

"You were saying something about us having some things in common, Bishop Dunne. Are some of your people Jewish?"

"Well, in a round about way, I guess you could say so. You see, according to our founder, Joseph Smith, it is stated in *The Book of Mormon*, that two lost tribes of Israel came to North America. He then proceeded to tell Otto the history of the two lost tribes and their relationship to their founder, Joseph Smith. Otto struggled to follow the thread of the story from the fast-talking bishop who was clearly enjoying his new company. "But that weren't all. Joseph Smith received many other divine revelations – one, of which, directed him to lead a movement to reclaim the Promised Land of the Nephites. And, like your Moses, our esteemed Prophet did not reach the land of Zion. He was murdered by a pack of gentiles a couple of years back in Illinois. Today, under the leadership of Brigham Young, we are carrying on Prophet Smith's work. Thousands of us have turned the wastelands of Utah territory into our very own Garden of Eden. The prophet Smith also believed that single women had a hard time of it, so he decreed that it would be acceptable to have more that one wife. I am married to Rose and Martha."

Otto looked over at White Feather and was relieved that she could not understand what Bishop Dunne had been saying. He realized that so many pioneers figured it their right to claim land from the Indians, that their way of life would soon come to an end. There was no doubt that the Mormons were nice people – taking them in and all, and he was grateful. But, Otto felt a surprising allegiance to Ghost Walker and the Indian girl. He decided it was time to go.

Otto thanked Martha for tending to his feet. She had wrapped them both in clean white cloth. He stood up and dusted the dirt off his pants. "I wish to thank you so much for being so kind to me and my *friend*. Otto stressed the word friend as he wanted the Mormons to know that White Feather meant more to him than just an Indian girl he had escaped with. "I would not want to get you mixed up in our troubles, so I think it is best that we be on our way. I must try and reach Fort Laramie before our wagon train pulls out, and we can make faster time riding the horses."

Bishop Dunne looked clearly disappointed. "Are ya sure? A lively young man such as yerself would be a big help to the Saints in Salt Lake City. Course, you'd have to part ways with yer Indian gal, here. But, as you probably noticed, there are plenty of young maidens in our midst for you to pair up with in marriage."

Otto's face turned flush with embarrassment. He could see that the bishop seemed in a rush to marry him off to one, or perhaps two, of his flock. "Thank you so much for this kind offer, but we must go... *now*."

"What are you going to do with the horses? The US Army don't take kindly to strangers riding across the prairie on their soldiers' horses."

Otto suddenly got uncomfortable thinking about the way the soldiers in Russia had treated his family, but decided that it was a chance he would have to take. "Once we get to Fort Laramie, we will leave the horses at the fort with the army soldiers. We will explain how we got them."

Bishop Dunne looked over at his wife and said, "Rosie, pack up some biscuits and hardtack for brother Otto here." Rose nodded and set to work filling a flour sack with some food. He then turned to his son. "Micah, fetch the horses."

"Yes, sir." Micah turned and seemed, to Otto, just a bit too eager for him to leave.

"You have been most nice to us, Bishop Dunne. If ever I am in Salt Lake City, I will be asking where you live. It would be my pleasure to do something nice for you to repay your kindness to us."

Rose and Martha walked over with a satchel of food and placed the sack in his hands. "I'll be praying that the Lord watches over ya, Otto," said Rose.

"Peace be with you, brother," added Martha.

Otto suddenly felt guilty that he was in such a hurry to leave Bishop Dunne and his hearty band of Mormons. They had been very kind to him, but he had the feeling that he and White Feather needed to get as far away from the territory as possible.

Bishop Dunne reached out for Otto's hand. "The Lord's blessing upon ya, brother Otto. You be careful and mind how you go."

"Thank you, sir." Otto motioned to White Feather. They mounted the army horses and gently urged them in the direction of the western horizon. Otto looked back over his shoulder and saw the two girls talking to Micah. He wondered if they were on the *hunt*.

Chapter 12 ~ June 1854 - Overland Trail

Otto and Little Feather found a shallow place to cross to the south side of the river and, they soon picked up the overland trail. It was easy to follow. Deep ruts cutting into the prairie from the heavy covered wagons defined the trail like tracks on a rail line. They rode until the sun dipped out of sight, and decided to stop for the night.

The pair found shelter in a gulley with a fast moving creek that ran through its lowest point. There was tender grass for the horses and the sack of food packed by Rose and Martha. They decided that it would be safe to make a small fire with a few matches given to him by Bishop Dunne, just to discourage unwanted wildlife like a cougar or a pack of coyotes. Otto's body shuddered at the thought of a facedown with another mountain lion. This time, there would be no Amethyst Bottle to help him. He knew that the shelter of the gulley would hide the small flame from the open prairie. The two were exhausted and had decided to catch up on their sleep and get an early start in the morning.

Otto watched as the Indian girl tended to the modest fire. He asked in Lakota, "What is the name of the ill-tempered brave with marks on his face?"

"He is called Black Wolf."

Otto could not think of the Lakota word for Pockface, so he decided not to mention the secret name he had made up for Black Wolf. Instead he offered, "Black Wolf was very fond of you."

"It is as you say, but my heart has always been with another."

Otto looked at the girl. Even in the soft light of the fire, it was easy to see the sadness on her face. He decided to change the subject. "What is your name?"

"After I was stolen from my village, the chief of the Crow gave me the name Snow Flower. He said I was like the fiery red flower that is so stubborn it can push its way through the winter snows to show itself."

"Do you like the name?"

"It is an honorable name, but now that I am free, I wish to be called by the name that was given to me by my mother and father."

"What name is this?"

"Among my people, I was called, Little Feather."

Otto laughed. "I do not mean to be impolite. It is only that…well, in the Crow camp I would call you White Feather in my mind because of the little white feather you always wear in your hair. I was close to the truth, yes?"

Little Feather reached up and gently touched the small white feather in her hair.

Otto continued. "It is odd though but perhaps a good sign. The Indian who taught me to speak the beautiful language of the Sioux also wore a small white feather in his hair. But there is something else that is most amazing. His pony carried this name because an unusual marking on its forehead. It looked like a tiny white feather floating in the wind."

White Feather became suddenly very animated and asked Otto, "What is the name of this Indian who taught you to speak the language of my people so well? Maybe I know him."

"His name is Ghost Walker and he is my friend," offered Otto proudly.

Otto watched as the girl's face fell like a withered autumn leaf. With sorrow in her voice she said, "There is no one by this name from my village. The name I was hoping to come to my ears above all others was…Gray Owl. Have you ever heard your friend speak this name?"

Otto hated to disappoint Little Feather. He could see she was crestfallen. "No. I am very sorry. My friend, Ghost Walker, has taught me many things, but he does not often talk about his life before he came to be a scout for Captain McAuliffe's wagon train. I only know that he was rescued by our captain, and he too had lost his family."

"It would have been too much to hope for."

"Was your friend in the village on the day you were taken?"

"No. He was not there that day."

"What happened to your family?"

"When I was a girl who had seen the warmth of thirteen summers, a band of Crow rode into our village. They destroyed everything and everyone. I was gathering berries for my mother just outside the encampment when angry men rode hard into our village with voices that pierced the air like mad wolves. I could hear the screams and cries from our people as I hid in the bushes and watched smoke coiling into the sky like a snake. When they had completed their punishment and were riding away with their stolen horses, I was found crouching in the bushes. Why they did not kill me, I do not know." Little Feather poked her stick in the fire. "I do not like to think back on that time."

Otto was at a loss for words to comfort Little Feather, so he shared his own experience of losing his family in Russia. Finally he said, "I think you should come with me to Fort Laramie. My friend Ghost Walker is a great scout who knows this land better than anyone. He may know something of your friend. I think he would be of a mind to help you."

Little Feather stared off into the night and for a minute Otto wondered if she had even heard him. At length, she looked across the small campfire and sighed. "I have nowhere else to go. It will be good to meet your friend and speak the language of my people with him."

Otto smiled and nodded his head in satisfaction.

Otto and Little Feather had been on the overland trail for four days. The food, given to them by Martha and Rose was long gone, but the sack had proved to be most useful. Little Feather made certain they did not go hungry. Otto watched with admiration as she continued to catch fish with her bear hands. Once she had used the sack like a net to capture tiny fish which she roasted on a rock until they turned crunchy when he put them in his mouth. Sometimes she would surprise him by filling the sack with berries or other strange tasting roots that grew inside the ground to roast over the fire each night. The two had seen no sign of Black Wolf or his Indian braves, and with each passing day they relaxed their guard.

As Otto sat on the sturdy Quarter Horse, that seemed well-suited for prairie life, he noticed that the land was changing. In the distance, he could see a large range of mountains that he assumed to be the Rockies. There were ever-growing signs that they were getting closer to Fort Laramie. Tattered notes, stuck into the branches of scraggly trees, told the friends and loved ones who would follow when they had passed along the trail and how long they would wait for them at the fort. Otto felt that each note held a story of the brave emigrants who traveled the overland trail.

Earlier in the morning, Otto and Little Feather had come across a family who had stocked up with supplies at Fort Laramie and were heading back east to their hometown in

Missouri. Over the past months, while heading west, the husband and wife had buried four of their five children at different points along the overland trail. The splintered family needed to go home so they could grieve their losses with the loved ones they had left behind. The young couple had been kind to Otto and Little Feather and offered up a few biscuits – along with some welcome information. They said that Fort Laramie was less than a day's ride in front of them. The husband reckoned that Otto and Little Feather would arrive at the fort late in the afternoon. Otto's heart swelled with happiness with the thought of catching up with Captain McAuliffe and the others on the wagon train. The strangers parted ways with wishes of better luck for the future.

Otto filled his nostrils with air. The afternoon was clear with a gentle breeze brushing against the riders' faces. To Otto, it was as though the wind was clearing away the unpleasant events of the past week. Out of the corner of his eye, a flash of purple color bounce off the westerly sun. The young rider caught his breath when he saw it – a yard of the uniquely-colored purple satin ribbon threaded tightly into the branches of a tall tree. Otto moved to the side of the road and shielded his eyes from the sun.

From its place, perched high in the tree, Otto could see that the ribbon would have discouraged most folks from taking the time to disentangle it from its spot. Otto caught his breath and coaxed his horse off the main road for a closer look. Little Feather slowed her horse to a halt and sat looking at Otto's unusual behavior. At first Otto was confused, and he briefly wondered if the twister could have carried the ribbon to its new place of confinement.

"Whoa," said Otto to his horse. "Steady, girl." The gentle brown mare was happy to stop and rest under the tree. Otto stretched his hands high overhead. He was surprised at the way his hands trembled in anxious anticipation as he reached up and pulled the branch down to eye-level. With care, Otto gently uncoiled the ribbon from its captivity. In the process, he could see the little ink-stained heart that Victoria had refused to have cut from its length. And then his heart leapt with joy! As he cradled the ribbon into his hands, he could see that it had not blown there by chance. Tiny little stitches had been sewn by loving hands to repair the small tears in the satin. Victoria had talked about that very thing the last time he had seen her on the prairie.

"Yes!" shouted Otto with joy.

"What is this thing you have found?" asked Little Feather.

"It is called a..." (Otto could not think of a Sioux word for ribbon). "Women wear them for decoration, like you wear your feather. It belongs to a friend of mine. I thought she was lost to me, but now I know she is alright. I think she left this ribbon along the trail for me to find."

Little Feather smiled at Otto. It was easy to share in his joy. Still, a part of her was sad and she wondered if she had made a mistake coming so far from her home to meet Otto's friend, Ghost Walker.

Chapter 13 ~ July 1854 - Fort Laramie

Fort Laramie was a bustling place. Built in 1834, it was first called, Fort William after William Sublette who ran the Rocky Mountain Fur Company. Near the original adobe building, a large wooden structure, fortified with high walls and gun turrets, housed soldiers and the many tradesmen who sold supplies to the emigrants at cutthroat prices. It was an impressive sight for the pioneers who drove their covered wagons in from the prairie. Otto suddenly felt overwhelmed by it all, and he could only imagine what Little Feather must be feeling. Scores of covered wagons rested around the perimeter of the outpost. In the distance, Otto could see a large number of Indians living in tipis which stuck up from the ground like a forest of coned-shaped paper hats.

A young soldier, with bright red hair and a mass of freckles on his face, suddenly left his post and marched over to Otto and Little Feather. The soldier was dressed in a blue army uniform and he carried a rifle with an imposing bayonet on its muzzle.

"Halt!" The young man's voice cracked, as if he hadn't quite found the right tone in his voice. He cleared his throat and demanded to know how Otto and the Indian girl came to be riding on a pair of army horses.

Otto started to speak but the soldier cut him off with a wave of his rifle. "Don't you be botherin' me with your sorry tale. Save your breath, lad, and tell it to the colonel." With that, the soldier took hold of the reins and walked Little Feather and Otto through the gates of the fort. Otto desperately scanned his eyes over the masses of people milling about, but saw no one that he recognized.

Colonel Lindstrom was accustomed to dealing with the multitude of problems that cropped up each day at Fort Laramie. Therefore, he was not overly surprised to see a boy in dirty clothing with no shoes and an Indian girl standing before him.

"What's the problem here, Private Dugan?"

Private Dugan saluted the captain and said, "I found these two ridin' into the fort on two army-issue horses, sir."

The colonel looked at Otto and asked, "Would you mind telling me how you came in possession of army horses?"

Otto gulped in a quantity of air and said, "I was captured by some Crow Indians ten days ago. This Sioux girl was also taken as a prisoner. While there, the braves who kept us against our will brought five horses into our camp one day. I could see the brands and knew right away that they were from the army. Some days ago, we were able to sneak out of the camp at night. We took with us two horses. I was planning to leave them here with you and then try and catch up with my wagon train, which I believe is gone from this fort and heading to California."

The colonel leaned forward, narrowed his eyes and tilted his head slightly to one side. "What was the name of wagon master of your outfit?"

Otto's face brightened and he said, "I work as a wrangler for Captain Cornelius P. McAuliffe."

The colonel sat back in his chair, scratched the back of his neck and asked, "Is your name Otto?"

"Yes, sir, I am Otto Stanoff." Then following the lead from Private Dugan, Otto put his hand to his forehead and saluted the captain.

Colonel Lindstrom laughed and excused Private Dugan by asking him to take the horses to the stables to be checked over.

"Mac has been bringing wagons into Fort Laramie for several years. His outfit rode out early the day before yesterday, but he left this for you." The captain opened the top drawer of his desk and pulled out an envelope. He handed it over to Otto. "Captain McAuliffe wanted me to give this letter to you if you showed up at the fort. He was anxious for you to have it. Said he or one of his men would check on his return trip to see if you had picked it up. I told him I'd be glad to hold the letter for him."

Otto looked down at the envelope bearing the name Otto Stanoff on the front, "May I open it here, Colonel Lindstrom?"

The colonel smiled and nodded.

Inside the envelope was a letter and four twenty-dollar gold coins. The twenty dollar gold pieces, called the double eagle, had been recently minted in 1849 and were in general circulation after 1850. Otto's eyes opened wide at the sight of the money. Slowly and with care, he began unfolding the letter. Otto looked down at the firm neat script of Cornelius P. McAuliffe.

> **Dear Otto,**
>
> **If you are reading this letter, it means that you have somehow found your way to Fort Laramie. Enclosed are your wages for working as my faithful and trusted employee. Buy yourself a horse and other supplies and hook up with another outfit as a wrangler to get to California. You may use this letter as a reference. I hope you find your brother but if that doesn't work out, look me up. You can always work for me.**
>
> **With kindest regards,**
>
> **Cornelius P. McAuliffe**

Colonel Lindstrom looked up at Otto and said, "Captain McAuliffe is a fine man, Otto, as I'm sure you already know. He seemed right-anxious for me to be on the lookout for you. I must admit though, I thought the captain looked mighty tired. But, then again, he's been at this business for quite some time now. He probably just needs a rest."

Otto felt slightly sick. He too had noticed the captain's drawn appearance in the last month. Otto looked at Colonel Lindstrom and said, "Thank you, sir."

"It's been my pleasure. Now, you'd best hide that money away in a safe place. There are masses of scoundrels at the fort who would love to take that gold off your hands. Go down to the stables and buy yourself a good horse and some hardtack. If you hurry, you should be able to catch up with your outfit just about the time they reach Independence Rock."

Otto nodded and placed the envelope in his pocket. Little Feather had stood quietly by, but she could tell that the meeting had gone well by the pleased expression on Otto's face. Otto turned to her and said in Lakota, "Come, we must buy a horse."

The colonel looked at Otto with a quizzical look and asked, "Is this Indian girl your wife?"

Now, it was Otto's turn to laugh. "This is the second time this week that I have been questioned about having a wife. I am not on a *hunt* for a wife, colonel. This is Little Feather, and she is my friend."

Bobby Wynn Harris was a con artist. For a while, he had worked with a traveling carnival where he tempted people to bet their hard-earned money on finding a pea under of one of three walnut shells he rotated around a table at lightning speeds. A quick smile set off a strong jaw line while a crop of thick blond hair drew attention to his boyishly handsome face. Bobby Wynn had been thrown out of many towns in Illinois and Missouri for selling phony elixirs, and posing as a minister while swindling money out of old ladies for fake charities. That, and an assortment of other shady operations had forced him to skedaddle west where he could start afresh. It might have been easy to see Bobby Wynn for what he really was – a charlatan, if it were not for the fact that he was so incredibly charming.

Bobby Wynn leaned against the fence of his corral and watched with fake-indifference as a young shoeless boy and a pretty Indian girl checked out the horses inside his corral. He adjusted his fancy brocade vest and bowler hat and sized up his cliental like a coyote waiting to tear into a rabbit. He wondered how much money he could squeeze out of the sorry-looking customers.

Most of his horses had been bought at rock-bottom prices from penniless pioneers heading west who desperately needed the money for supplies for their families. Usually, the horses were old and on their last leg, or they possessed a wild streak that made them difficult to ride. Bobby Wynn shined the horses' coats with shoe polish to make the horses look pretty, but on the inside they were mostly worn out.

Bobby Wynn strolled over to Otto and Little Feather and asked, "Lookin' for a horse?"

"Yes," said Otto.

"Well my friends, you've come to the right place." Bobby Wynn stuck out his hand and smiled. Talking so fast that Otto could hardly keep up his banter, Bobby Wynn said, "Let me introduce myself. I am Bobby Wynn Harris at your service. Now, I hate to part with her, but I can make you a fine deal on that good-looking brown mare standing in the center with the diamond marking on her forehead. And, remember my motto friends. *You'll ride out with a grin, when you buy a horse from Bobby Wynn.*"

Otto and Little Feather could see that, despite their shiny coats, most of the horses had medical problems and would not be worth much. They had already picked out a young black and brown pony standing off in the corner by itself. Little Feather was certain that the pony probably belonged to an Indian. The young colt looked to be about three-years-old and had no brand on his hide or horseshoes on its feet.

"How much do you want for the black and brown pony in the corner?"

Bobby Wynn smiled as he spoke. "Now that's a fine piece of horseflesh, young man. I bought him off a fur trapper only yesterday. He's a fiery one though. So far no one's been able to ride him. The horse just won't take to a saddle. I can let him go for forty dollars."

Otto had spent too many hours bargaining for food in Five Points and he was more than ready for a face-off with Bobby Wynn Harris. He turned to Little Feather and asked in Lakota, "The man says the pony is hard to ride. If you think we can ride him, I will barter for a price."

Little Feather looked over at the horse and nodded her head.

"I am just a poor boy as you can plainly see. I go to California to hunt for gold, but someone stole my shoes and other belongings. Please, sir, would you take ten dollars for a horse no one can ride?"

"I'll tell you what, kid. Give me twenty dollars and you've got a deal."

Otto gave Bobby Wynn a forlorn look of sadness. "I guess it was too much to hope for. Now, I must walk to California." Otto took Little Feather's hand and walked away. Bobby Wynn watched as the boy's shoulders slumped forward and dust flew up and settled on the bottom of his torn pants from his bare feet.

Otto had walked about twenty yards when Bobby Wynn called him back.

"You drive a hard bargain kid. Fifteen dollars and you've got a deal."

Otto turned around and walked back to where the horse trader stood and held out his hand. "Throw in a halter and I agree. Shake on it?"

"Oh hell's fire, kid, you'll probably get thrown to the ground by the ornery beast before you leave the fort." With that, he shook Otto's hand.

Bobby Wynn Harris was a man who rarely got ruffled, but when he saw Otto reach into to an envelope and pull out a twenty dollar gold-piece he almost dropped to the dirt.

Otto smiled innocently at the stunned conman and asked, "Can you give me correct change for this coin?"

As Bobby Wynn reached into his pocket he said, "It doesn't happen often, but you hoodwinked me, kid." He handed Otto a five dollar gold-piece and tipped his hat to the victor.

Otto and Little Feather bought buffalo jerky, a new tin of matches, and two woolen blankets for five dollars. As they walked the pony out past the encampment of Indians, Little Feather traded one of the skins of water for a new pair of moccasins for Otto. They decided to use the remaining light of the day to get as close to Independence Rock as possible. Now the only question was would they be able to ride the horse? Little Feather moved around to face the pony. She breathed into its nostrils and whispered soft words in the language of her people. The girl's actions reminded Otto of the first day that he had met Ghost Walker – an incident that seemed so far in the past. After a measure of time, Little Feather told Otto that the horse was ready for riding. Otto watched as Little Feather mounted the horse with the ease of graceful swan. Otto pulled himself up behind the girl and the pony trotted gently down the path with the late afternoon sun on their faces.

Chapter 14 ~ July 1854 - Independence Rock

Formed from granite, the enormous rock looked like a giant beached whale. A party of fur trappers, who camped there on July 4, 1824, had named the popular monument to honor American Independence Day. Legend stated that a wagon train had to reach the rock before the fourth of July to have enough time to cross over the mountains before the winter snows arrived. Over the years, many pioneers had scratched their names into the granite or used axel grease or tar.

The wagon train had pulled in around noon and Captain McAuliffe informed the members that they would camp in the shadow of the rock for the rest of the day and begin their march again in the morning – a trek that would take them through South Pass and on to Fort Bridger.

The Englishman, Sir Nigel Churchstone, asked the captain if they might celebrate the occasion with a dance that evening. He offered up his butler, Simon Walton, who had twice before entertained the members with music from his fiddle. McAuliffe smiled and nodded his head. It was good to see the group in a festive spirit.

The mood in the camp had been low since Otto had disappeared during the twister. Luckily, the wagon train had suffered only minor damages during the storm. The members had rejoiced to see Victoria Dickerson stagger into camp, but an intense search of the area for Otto proved futile. Ghost Walker had found some Indian tracks in the area with a trail heading north. He had wanted to follow their path, but Mac felt an obligation to the pioneers to keep the wagons moving west.

Victoria climbed to the top of the rock, with the ease of a cat, to look at the many names left by those heading west. The persistent cough that had plagued her for years seemed a thing of the past. She found a smooth section of rock, dropped to her knees, and pulled out her bottle of India ink and a small paintbrush from her apron pocket. With tears streaming down her cheeks, she reverently printed out the names in neat letters:

Otto Stanoff ~ Victoria Dickerson
July 3 ~ 1854

Victoria bowed her head and whispered, "Wherever you are, Otto, I hope you are safe and will somehow find your way back to us. Until then, I will keep your beloved bottle safely by my side. Future people who pass this way will know that you made this trip in 1854."

With the wind to her back Victoria sat next to the inscription and looked down at the trail leading into Independence Rock. The late afternoon sun felt warm on her shoulders as she removed the Amethyst Bottle from its case and sighed. She looked at the patch of violet that reminded her of the color of her satin ribbon and wondered if it had been foolish to ask Papa to pull the wagon up to the tall tree so she could wrap her ribbon around its branches. The girl had grieved for days over the loss of her friend, and somehow the gesture helped ease the sadness in her heart.

Suddenly, Victoria felt an energy coming from inside the bottle. The power sent a tingling sensation up her arms and inside her body. The vibration unnerved her and she placed the bottle next to the inscription on the rock. Then, something drew her eyes to a painted pony trotting along the trail that led into their camp. Two riders shared the horse. Victoria caught her breath and froze. One of the riders waved his hand in the air.

Victoria stood up and shouted in the direction of the oncoming pony.

"Otto, look this way. It's Victoria." She knew her friend had heard her when he unfurled the unusual purple ribbon into the air from his hand. It snapped smartly in the breeze like a cavalry flag. Victoria's heart soared, and she quickly placed the bottle in its case and gathered the other things into her hands to make her way down the back of the granite whale.

A crowd of chattering people had gathered around Otto and the Indian girl but parted to let Victoria through. The usually shy girl surprised Otto by flinging herself into his arms. Chandler let out a howl and everyone laughed in unison.

Victoria's eyes were still wet with tears when she declared, "You found the ribbon! I put it there for you hoping it would lead you back to us."

Otto looked at his friend and said, "This ribbon gave me hope that I would see you all again."

At that moment, Captain McAuliffe made his way through the circle of people. He looked at Otto dressed in dirty clothes and a pair of moccasins and laughed. "Well, Otto, you're a sight for sore eyes."

The smile on Otto's face sank as he asked, "Do your eyes hurt to see me, Captain McAuliffe? I would never want to cause you pain."

Mac let out a roar of laughter and said, "No, Otto, these eyes have never been happier to see anyone. I must say though, you look like you've been wrestling with a bear. Who's your companion?"

"This is my friend, Little Feather. She helped me escape from a band of Indians. Where Is Ghost Walker? I was hoping to introduce her to him."

"Ghost Walker and Kirby are out hunting for meat. I expect them back shortly. We're planning a little celebration tonight. Now, I guess we really have something to kick up our heels about. Speaking of which, what happened to your shoes?"

"They are now warming the feet of an Indian woman." Everyone laughed again.

Isaac Wise took a step forward and announced, "Otto, I will make you a new pair of boots from my finest leather."

"Thank you Mr. Wise, and thanks to Captain McAuliffe, I can pay." Otto reached into his pocket and pulled out the captain's letter and three twenty dollar gold pieces.

Isaac waved his hand, "Oh no, Otto, the shoes will be my gift to you."

McAuliffe looked at the three shiny coins with admiration. "I'd be pleased to hold that money for you, Otto, until we reach California. Otto happily handed the coins over to Mac as the captain pointed to the pony and added. "Looks like you made the better part of a trade with the missing twenty dollar gold piece."

Otto looked over at Victoria and beamed. "I'm going to call my new pony Hawkeye after the scout of my favorite author, James Fennimore Cooper."

Victoria removed the leather strap from her shoulder and handed the Amethyst Bottle over to Otto. "I have been saving this for you. It's helped me a lot, but it belongs to you."

Otto gathered the bottle into his hands and placed it over his shoulder. Otto felt the faint sensation of purring as it nestled against his side. He smiled. It felt good to be back in the circle of friends.

Ghost Walker and Kirby rode into camp with five wild turkeys and four rabbits. They had hoped to bring down a deer, but knew any meat would be a welcome addition to the evening's festivities.

Kirby offered to take the meat to some of the women who would roast the catch for the common dinner they would share before the dance.

Ghost Walker nodded, slipped off his pony, and walked over to Biscuit's campfire. He stopped in his tracks when he saw Otto, sitting on a rock near the campfire, finishing up a plate of sourdough flapjacks smothered in Biscuit's prized apple butter. Otto was chattering away to Captain McAuliffe. A big smile on the captain's face impelled Otto to turn around. Standing before him was Ghost Walker. Otto leapt up from the rock and almost dumped the tin plate into the fire. McAuliffe reached out and grabbed the plate thereby averting disaster. Otto stretched out his hands as he walked over to Ghost Walker.

As the two embraced, Otto said in Lakota, "It warms my heart to look into the face of my good friend once more. There were times when I wondered if we would ever see each other again."

Ghost Walker smiled. Otto thought how handsome he looked. Then, he realized that in all the time the two had spent together on the plains, he had never seen his friend smile before.

Ghost Walker stated respectfully, "Brother, my spirit soars like an eagle to hear Otto say the Sioux words once more. Otto seems to speak Lakota even better than before we parted ways."

Now it was Otto's turn to say with pride. "It is because of my new friend, Little Feather. I brought her here to meet you…." Otto's voice suddenly trailed off when he saw the color drain from Ghost Walker's face.

Ghost Walker looked frantically around the camp. Thinking he may have not understood, he asked again, "What is this name you speak?"

"Little Feather. She has gone down to the water to wash her face...." Again, Otto stopped before he could finish his words. McAuliffe and Otto watched Ghost Walker race in the direction of the water.

Little Feather knelt on a large flat rock and looked into the pool of water. A single tear distorted the reflection of her face on its surface. When the image of her features reappeared, the girl stared down at a face filled with sadness.

Otto's friends had been nice enough to her, but Little Feather felt lost and alone. She reflected on whether it had been wise to leave her Crow family. *No,* she thought, *I could not stay with the ones who had killed my parents and destroyed my childhood.* Little Feather hoped that Otto's friend Ghost Walker would help her find another tribe of Sioux who would take her in.

She had long since finished cleaning her face and hands and knew that Otto would start to worry about her if she tarried too long, but something kept her planted on the rock. She needed time to gather her strength to face what lay ahead for her future.

Lost in her thoughts, Little Feather did not notice the faint sound of footsteps come up on the rock from behind. Nor did the girl jump or move when another face suddenly appeared next to her reflection in the water. Something vaguely familiar about the face put her calmly at peace. Little Feather felt almost like she was dreaming – of another time when she was but a girl on the edge of womanhood.

She caught her breath when the voice whispered softly into her ear, "How did the wind come to carry my Little Feather home to me?"

Little Feather's throat formed a lump, and the tears that fell from her eyes distorted the faces in the water. "Is this a dream? Could it be you, Gray Owl?"

Two strong hands touched her shoulders and the voice answered, "It is as you say, Little Feather. You have found your way to me, and I will never let you go."

Little Feather felt like she was floating as two muscular hands lifted her gently from the rock to her feet. Gray Owl turned Little Feather around and pulled her into his chest. Little Feather grasped Gray Owl around the neck and buried her face into his shoulder. On this rock, Little Feather and Gray Owl embraced as one. On this rock, the two childhood friends shed tears of sadness and tears of joy.

At length, Gray Owl cupped the face of Little Feather into his hands and said, "You have grown more beautiful than the young girl who has haunted my dreams. The image of that girl always left me filled with sadness with the rising of the sun."

"It has been the same for me too, Gray Owl." Suddenly, Little Feather sensed that they were no longer alone. She turned to see a startled look on Otto's face, as though he had seen a ghost.

Otto asked Little Feather in Lakota, "Do you know my friend, Ghost Walker?"

"I know your friend, Otto, but his name is not Ghost Walker."

"Is this true, Ghost Walker?"

For the second time that day, Otto saw his friend smile. "Yes, Otto, it is as Little Feather says. My Sioux name is Gray Owl."

Simon Walton plucked the strings of his violin with added enthusiasm. The music seemed to reflect the mood of everyone in the camp. Dust flew up from the dirt floor of the dance area as the members stepped to the rhythm of the music. A large bonfire spilled light onto the celebration. Captain McAuliffe watched Otto and Victoria whirl amidst the other dancers as he sat with Gray Owl and Little Feather.

He looked at the Indians and said, "It's going to take me some time to get used to calling you Gray Owl. I always wondered what your real name was after you decided to keep the name I had given you when you were a boy. On that dark day back at your ruined village, I knew that the boy had become a man."

Gray Owl held Little Feather's hand and said, "Gray Owl died that day in my village, but with Otto finding Little Feather, young boy is dead no more." Gray Owl looked over at the captain and continued. "If we were in village, my father, a respected shaman, would join us together as man and woman. Sadly, that can never come to pass. I have seen you join other people in ceremony you call *wedding*. I know my father would have respected you as Gray Owl respects you now. I humbly ask if you would say words of your people to join Little Feather and Gray Owl together for all time."

Cornelius P. McAuliffe rarely let his emotions get the better of him. Tonight they would. Maybe it was having young Otto back. Perchance it was finally seeing the long awaited joy on the face of his valued scout. Therefore, the members were a little surprised when he burst into the center of the dance floor and shouted, "Stop the music, Mr. Walton!" Gradually the dancing slowed to a stop and everyone looked in the direction of the captain. "This is a fine night for celebration indeed." He pointed over to Gray Owl and Little Feather and exclaimed, "Tonight, we're going to have a wedding!"

Amid the clapping and shouting, only Otto noticed Bull standing outside the perimeter of the party with a scowl on his face. He watched as Bull spat in the dirt and skulked away into the darkness.

Chapter 15 ~ July 1854 - South Pass

The wagon train followed the Sweetwater River to a canyon known as Devil's Gate. The members passed alongside the monument which brought them to South Pass. It was here that they would cross the Rocky Mountains. McAuliffe called everyone for a meeting.

"This next patch will be a smooth stretch for the oxen. Crossing over the Rockies through South Pass, you'll encounter a gentle grade that is over twenty miles wide. When we reach the summit of the *Great Divide* all the rivers will flow west instead of east. Barring any unforeseen circumstances, we should arrive at Fort Bridger in around five days."

Otto was pleased to be back working with the horses for the wagon train. He spent every spare minute grooming his new pony, Hawkeye. Gray Owl had given the stallion a thorough going-over, and he reckoned the horse to be four-years-old. McAuliffe had promised to help Otto purchase a saddle when they reached Fort Bridger. He said it would be up to Otto to convince the steed to want to wear it.

Gray Owl and Little Feather were very happy. Julia Dickerson and a few of the other ladies had donated some of their clothes to Little Feather. Isaac Wise and his family offered them a beautiful lambskin rug to sleep on. Sir Nigel surprised them with a sturdy little canvas tent as a wedding present, which they slept in each night. He said he had planned to use the tent once he got to the gold fields, but would buy another one when he reached San Francisco.

It always amazed Otto at the stylish manner in which the Englishman and his man-servant, Simon, traveled. Unlike most of the other pioneers, Sir Nigel appeared to possess a great deal of money. His wagon was equipped with every known amenity for traveling in style and comfort. Otto once asked him why he left England to make such a difficult trip across the wilderness to California.

Sir Nigel had answered, "I was utterly bored living on my estate outside London. I filled my days with fox hunts, costume balls, and endless tea parties with the same tiresome people. I have always been fascinated with America, and I wanted a slice of adventure. I love the open spaces where a man can breathe free. Why, young Otto, I'm having the time of my life! It's not about finding the gold. It will be the thrill of hunting for it! Oh, I'll go back to England in a year or so. I'll marry the young girl to whom I am promised and take my place in polite society. But now, I'm exploring this new-fangled land. By Jove, I'll have countless stories to tell to my grandchildren."

Gray Owl and Little Feather had informed the captain that they would be leaving the wagon train at the end of the season. It seemed that Gray Owl had spent very little of the money he had made working as a scout for the captain. He had asked the captain to keep it in a safe place for him. So McAuliffe had placed the scout's money in a bank in San Francisco. It had been drawing interest over the years, and McAuliffe told him that he possessed a sizable little nest egg. Gray Owl had been living among white people long enough to know that the traditions of his people and other tribes of the plains were sadly coming to an end. Mac encouraged him to buy some land from the government to insure that he and his family would not ever be moved onto an Indian reservation. Gray Owl listened and said he would consider the captain's advice.

Just as McAuliffe had predicted, the trail over the Rocky Mountains was wide and smooth causing little trouble for the oxen. The members were making good time and spirits were high because everyone knew that when they reached Fort Bridger the outfit would be over half way to California.

They crossed over the summit known a the *Great Divide* and Otto noticed that it was as the captain had told them. Now the rivers were running down the western slope of the mountain. Otto felt his spirits pulled along with the westward flow of water that would carry him to his brother, Ivan.

McAuliffe circled the wagons near a river and told the outfit to get a good night's rest before crossing the swift-moving current in the morning.

Isaac Wise walked over to the captain's fire. Little Feather and the men were eating Biscuit's dinner. The little cobbler carried a cloth sack in his hands. "Pardon the interruption of your dinner, Captain."

Mac waved Isaac over to the fire and said, "Please, Mr. Wise, come and join us for a cup of coffee. We're just finishing up."

"Thank you, Captain, but I promised my three little girls that I would take them to look for wildflowers to add to their collection. We have catalogued over one hundred varieties thus far. I will not stay long. I just wanted to give this to Otto." A grin spread over Isaac's face as he handed the sack to Otto.

Otto opened the bag and pulled out a beautiful pair of sturdy riding boots. The boots were made from a soft, yet surprisingly thick brown leather that rose up mid-calf. Otto looked at Mr.

Wise and said, "Mr. Wise, these boots are most beautiful, May I try them on?"

Isaac beamed with pride at his handiwork and replied, "By all means."

Otto sat down and pulled off the moccasins. He had been surprised at how comfortable and practical the Indian shoes had been. Otto had been so busy, he had almost forgotten that the cobbler had traced a pattern of his feet onto paper shortly after he had returned to the wagon train. Mr. Wise told Otto that he was going to make the boots a little big to offset Otto's growth spurts, which seemed to continue with each passing week. Otto slipped the boots on and stood up to show them off. They fit well and felt comfortable. A huge grin spread across his face as he paraded around the campfire.

Bull, who had been quietly sipping on a tin mug of coffee snickered and said, "You look like a greenhorn, boy, in them new ridin' boots. You'll want to break them in fast or people will be callin' ya a dandy-boy." The trail hand set off to laughing at his own joke.

Otto turned to Isaac and uttered, "Thanks you Mr. Wise. I am certain that the gold miners will be standing in line to buy your beautiful boots in California."

"Yes, Otto, wouldn't that be wonderful!"

The next morning, Otto was angry to wake up to find his new boots filled with wet sand. Someone had gone to a great deal of trouble to take them from inside the wagon and fill them with damp sand from the river and replace them at the bottom of his bed. Otto knew that Bull had come to bed late after standing his shift at guard duty. It would have been easy for him to remove them from their place by his bunk to inflict mischief. The problem was he had no way to prove it.

Otto didn't want to be late for work, so he put on his moccasins and ran to saddle the horses for the day's ride. When he brought the horses over to the men who were eating breakfast, McAuliffe asked, "Where are your new boots, Otto? Thought for sure you'd be itching to try them out this morning."

Otto looked straight at Bull who had been quietly smirking into his tin of coffee and announced, "Someone put wet sand in my new boots as I slept last night. It is not the only time this has happened to me with new shoes."

Bull stood up and took a step toward Otto. "Why're you lookin' at me? Did you see me take yer shoes?"

Otto replied honestly, "No."

"Best you not go around accusing folks unless you have proof. Ya might get more than ya bargained for."

Otto stood his ground and added, "I did not see who took the boots, but not many knew they had been delivered to me by Mr. Wise. This snake would have to be someone from this camp. Who else would have the cunning to take them from the captain's own wagon?"

Kirby wiped his face with the back of his sleeve and said, "I woke up sometime last night and heard Bull rousting around in the wagon, but I just figured that he was looking for something."

Bull shot Kirby an angry glance. He looked over at Otto, stood up and said, "I'm not saying it were me, but even if it were, what's so wrong in havin' a little fun. Maybe you'd like to make somethin' of it!" Otto planted his feet when Bull stepped forward and doubled up his fists like he wanted to fight.

As Otto stared eye-level at Bull, he realized that he had grown so much over the past months that he was nearly as tall as the ornery trail hand. He also shrewdly noted that Bull probably outweighed him by fifty pounds. Still he stood his ground and said, "I do not wish trouble, but I will be more watchful from now on."

Cornelius P. McAuliffe sat back quietly and let the two hash it out. Quarrels happened from time to time when the men got edgy. He found that it was better to step in only as a last resort. Still, he did not like bullies, and he did not like them picking on ones who were not their equal in stature. The captain stood up and tossed the last few drops of coffee into the fire. "It's time to get this train moving, boys. We've got a job of work ahead of us trying to nudge these wagons across the river."

Mac had hired Bull only a year ago, and he had already made up his mind that he would be letting him go once they reached California. He just didn't fit in like Kirby and Gray Owl. There had been several times when he had quietly observed Bull goading Gray Owl, but the Indian had always seemed able to sidestep an outright confrontation by ignoring him. Then, yesterday, he had noticed Bull trying to get just a little too friendly with Little Feather while she was washing some clothes down by the river. He had pulled the cowboy aside and gave him a warning. Little Feather seemed shaken and Mac wondered if she would tell Gray Owl. When no words were exchanged between the two men, McAuliffe figured that Little Feather had not said anything to Gray Owl.

Otto was still angry as he brushed the sand from the inside of his new boots with his hands. The company had crossed the river with little trouble and had stopped for the nooning meal.

Otto desperately wanted to wear the new boots in the afternoon. He knew that Bull had probably messed with them and swore to himself that he would be extra careful in the future.

Otto tried to erase his anger when he saw Victoria come up where he sat in the shade of Biscuit's wagon. She carried a can and a cloth in her hands. "Chandler said that you were cleaning some sand out of your new boots. Thought maybe, I might be of some help to you. Pa loaned me some of his boot polish."

Otto looked up at his friend and blushed. Ever since coming back to camp after the tornado, he had begun to feel all tangled up inside when Victoria was around – like there was a small twister inside his belly.

"I...would like that," he said fumbling with his words. Otto noticed that Victoria wore a pale yellow dress with small white dots. The color complimented the healthy rosy-color of her cheeks and strawberry-blond hair. The violet satin ribbon in her hair enhanced her appearance, and Otto thought she looked as lovely as a field of wildflowers. He lowered his eyes and continued to scrape the sand from inside his new boots.

Victoria settled onto the grass next to him and picked up one of the boots. She removed the last traces of sand and began to expertly apply the boot polish to the brown leather. "We'll have these as good as new in no time."

Suddenly Otto froze. He stared at his friend and uttered. "You know, once before when we were waiting to leave Elm Grove someone spoiled my shoes with wet sand. I asked Mrs. Dickerson if I could dry them out on the seat of your wagon. The next day, when I went to fetch them, they were cleaned and polished – and I never knew who did that for me. Were you that kind person?"

Victoria did not look up from her task of polishing the boots and Otto thought that the rosy color in her cheeks grew a little brighter. She spoke softly, "I could see from my place in the wagon how upset you were as you walked over to our camp. I figured there was more to your story of telling Mama that you fell in the stream. I just wanted to do something nice for you. I never thought you'd find out it was me."

Otto placed his hand over Victoria's and she stopped polishing the boot. "I wish to thank you now for that kind deed. Back then, I was very much scared to be coming on this wagon train." Otto looked over at his friend until she returned his gaze. "That one act of kindness gave me the courage to make this trip west with Mr. McAuliffe, because I knew that there was someone making this journey who cared about me."

"It was really nothing."

"To you perhaps it was nothing. To me, it meant a great deal."

Otto almost jumped out of his moccasins when he heard Mac and Kirby yelling down the line, "Five minutes 'til wagon ho!"

Chapter 16 ~ July 1854 - Fort Bridger

Otto wondered why his mouth was as dry as a rock yet his palms were sticky with sweat. He tried to swallow and nervously looked around the corral to see several members of the wagon train watching him from outside the fence.

Bull threw the new saddle blanket over the pony and grunted, "Try not to break yer neck, greenhorn!" He laughed as he walked away.

Otto placed the saddle over Hawkeye's back. The pony skittered sideways and shook its head. Gray Owl held the horse's mouth in his hands and continued to whisper soft Lakota words into its face. Otto tightened the belt under the horse's belly and adjusted the stirrups. Hawkeye tried to rear up but Gray Owl held him down. In the background Otto heard words of encouragement from some of the people.

"Good luck to you, young Otto," yelled Isaac Wise.

"Stiff upper lip and all, Otto. We're pulling for you, chap!" shouted Sir Nigel Churchstone and his butler, Simon Walton.

Out of the corner of his eye, Otto could see Victoria standing next to Chandler who was shouting something about riding like a real cowboy.

Then, over the throng of noise, Otto heard Bull say, "Try not to git them new boots trampled under the horse's hooves when ya fall off, Jew boy."

Otto winced at the insult and looked at Gray Owl, "Would you hold my bottle for me? If I do fall, I don't want to break it." He gently removed the leather strap from his side and handed the bottle over to his friend.

Gray Owl took the bottle into his hands. He held Otto in his gaze. "Otto once make great kill. Lakota believe that spirit of *igmu* now lives inside you. Do not fear. The energy of the beast will help you complete your quest."

Otto nodded, sucked in a gulp of air, and slid his left foot in the stirrup.

Fort Bridger was the brainstorm of James Bridger. The famous mountain man wanted to cash in on the success of Fort Laramie. But unlike Fort Laramie, the privately owned fort built in 1843 from poles and mud, was a poor comparison. However, there was a decent blacksmith, a fine corral, and a respectable-enough supply of clothes and other goods that keep the wagon trains veering south to pass through its gates.

Captain McAuliffe trusted Jim and regarded him as a friend. Therefore he knew that Jim would give Otto the best deal possible on a saddle.

"I traded this here saddle for forty pounds of buffalo hardtack to a Mormon outfit that came through last month on their way to Salt Lake City. The leather's worn in a few places but the straps and stirrups are sound. I can letcha have it, Mac, for twenty-five dollars."

McAuliffe smiled and said, "Now that's a fair price, Jim, but Otto here's a might limited in funds. Could you see fit to part with it for fifteen?"

Bridger scratched the hair under his chin and countered, "I'll tell you what, Mac, because you're a friend of mine and bring me a fair parcel of business, I'll let it go for twenty."

"Throw in a new saddle blanket and brush and we'll call it a deal. Shall we shake on it?"

Bridger spat on the packed-dirt floor of his trading store and stuck out his hand. "You know your getting the best of me."

"I know, Jim, but you'll make it up on the next unfortunate pioneer."

Bridger laughed as the two sealed the deal with a handshake.

Otto eased his right leg over Hawkeye's back and lowered himself into the saddle. Before he could get settled, the pony reared up on his front legs and threw Otto to the ground. A roar of laughter erupted from the crowd. From his place on his backside and through the dust, Otto could see Captain McAuliffe close his eyes and grimace. Otto was not hurt and jumped up and brushed the dirt off his pants. He desperately wanted to please the captain and make a good impression with the new saddle.

Bull let out a loud whistle and shouted, "Watch yer step there, greenhorn!" He then howled with laughter.

Gray Owl had already rounded up the pony and was standing in the center of the corral whispering soothing words to the horse.

Otto thanked Gray Owl and patted the horse on its neck. "Come on, Hawkeye. Be a good pony. The saddle won't hurt you." The steed looked at the rider and snorted through his nose. Otto mounted the horse again and instantly found himself tossed to the floor of the corral like an apple core. This time, the fall was harder and Otto gasped for breath as the wind was knocked out of him. Otto struggled to his knees and prayed that he would have the courage to continue to break the Indian pony so it would want to take the saddle.

Amid hoots and hollers from the crowd, Otto noticed Bull laughing so hard he almost fell off the wooden fence of the corral. Otto gritted his teeth with determination and slowly stood up. He marched over to his pony and grabbed the reins from Gray Owl, all the while vowing that he would not become the laughing stock of the fort.

Otto was about to mount the horse for the third time when Gray Owl stopped him. The Indian wrinkled his forehead and suggested that they remove the saddle and blanket to make certain the job had been done properly. Otto was about to argue that he knew how to saddle a horse, but decided to let the Indian have his way. It would allow him the chance to compose himself before trying again.

Gray Owl continued to talk in soothing tones to the pony as Otto removed the saddle and blanket. Otto gasped when he observed the problem. Several thorny burrs were embedded into the new saddle blanket. Otto felt certain he had checked the new blanket inside the store. Then he remembered that Bull had offered to carry it over to the corral. Otto swore Bull's name under his breath. He was about to march over to the fence to confront his adversary when he felt the stony grip of Gray Owl's hand on his wrist.

"Otto must free mind of all things. Go on with training horse. When you have mastered this quest, we will look to our problems with Bull."

Otto nodded and suddenly felt empowered and somewhat relieved that Gray Owl had said *we*. With care, Otto carefully removed the thorny impediments from the blanket. He saddled the horse again and stepped around to look into the face of his pony. The horse's eyes seemed frightened and he tried to pull away from Otto's grasp. Suddenly an idea popped into Otto's head. He looked over at Gray Owl and noticed that the Indian was wearing his Amethyst Bottle strapped over his shoulder in its leather case.

"Gray Owl, may I borrow my bottle? Hawkeye may be thirsty."

Gray Owl slowly nodded his head and began to remove the bottle from its case and said, "There is much strength in this bottle. Energy spreads inside me like warmth of the sun that soaks into earth each morning."

Gray Owl removed the stopper and poured a measure of water into Otto's cupped hands. Hawkeye sniffed the water in Otto's hands then lapped up the liquid with his tongue. Otto repeated the effort twice more. When Otto decided to stop, Hawkeye made eye contact with the rider and snorted through his nostril. This time, when Otto gazed at the horse, he sensed a degree of calm. Otto turned to his Indian friend and said. "Let us begin the lesson once more."

With gentle motions, Otto mounted the saddle and held his breath. Hawkeye took a few steps backwards then came to a stop. This time, Gray Owl was able to hold onto the horse's head and reassure the pony with soft words. The ears of the horse seemed to slacken and Otto could feel the tension in the muscles of the pony relax. Gray Owl stepped away from the pony and nodded his head at Otto.

"Giddy-up, boy." Otto let out a sigh of relief when the horse shifted into a gentle walk and let Otto guide him around the interior of the corral. A roar of cheering and applause went up from the people gathered around the fence. Otto looked over at Victoria and returned her smile. He walked Hawkeye around the corral and then prompted him to a trot. The horse responded like a veteran. When it was clear that Hawkeye had adjusted to the saddle, Otto motioned for Gray Owl to take the horse's reins. He jumped down and stormed over to the fence to confront Bull.

People sensed that something was about to take place, and a hush fell over the crowd. Otto looked up at Bull who was still sitting on the fence of the corral. "You put sharp burrs in the horse's blanket on purpose! You put sand and water in my new shoes. These things are mean and I want you to stop!"

Bull jumped down from the fence and snickered as he stood before Otto. "You can't prove nothin', Jew boy. Even so, what if I did? Do you think yer man enough to stop me from havin' a little fun?"

Cornelius P. McAuliffe stubbed out the end of his cigarette on the heel of his boot and walked over to Otto and Bull. He looked at Bull and remarked, "Usually, I let you boys sort out your difference among yourselves, but you're not going to pick a fight with a boy you outweigh by two twenty-five-pound sacks of potatoes. Did you do the things he accuses you of?"

Bull looked up at the tall trail boss. The stern set of his Boss's jaw line told him that McAuliffe was as agitated as the horse with burrs in its blanket. A bit of the sting left Bull's voice when he answered, "Maybe, maybe not."

At that moment, Gray Owl walked up to Captain McAuliffe and said, "This not fair fight with man and boy, but this fair fight with man and Gray Owl. Many times I have turned my back from man who picks at others like buzzard. Now Gray Owl wish to challenge coward to fight. I fight for boy's honor, for wife's honor, and for Gray Owl's honor."

Cornelius P. McAuliffe bit down on his lower lip and wondered if White Feather *had* said something to Gray Owl after all. He knew she must have played the incident down or Gray Owl would not have had the patience to wait as long as he did to confront Bull. He turned to Bull and said, "Looks like you've been annoying more than a few members of my wagon train. Do you accept Gray Owl's challenge?"

"There ain't a redskin alive that I couldn't whip with one arm tied behind my back. I been wonderin' fer a long time if'n his skin really weren't red but yeller."

McAuliffe looked at the Indian who seemed unruffled by the racist comments and wondered how many times his scout had been abused with the callused sting of harsh words. The trail hand questioned if Gray Owl would be up to the task of winning a fist fight with a man who carried the bulk of Bull. McAuliffe noted that the Indian was taller than the short stocky cowboy, but Mac reckoned that Bull must outweigh him by at least thirty pounds. He shook his head in resignation and turned to Jim Bridger who had been standing alone on the opposite side of the corral.

"Jim, mind if we use your corral for settling a dispute among my men?"

Bridger, who stood lazily scratching his back with a stick replied, "Go right ahead, Mac. Won't be the first time the corral has been used to straighten out a brawl. The dirt's soft enough for landing seeing it's been kicked up by the horse's hooves. One of yer boys might end up in a pile of horse manure, but that'll just add a little amusement for the audience. I just wish I could charge admission to the show." Then, the crusty mountain man exploded into laughter, and some of the people gathered around the corral began to laugh too.

Otto looked at Gray Owl and started to protest, but the Indian cut his words off by saying, "This man has been like the point of an arrowhead in my backside for long time. It is fitting I should be first to set on right path." Gray Owl gently removed the Amethyst Bottle from his shoulder and handed it back to Otto. He added, "I feel strong spirit lives in this bottle. Spirit will guide me to victory in quest."

Otto gathered the bottle into his hands. "Gray Owl, you spoke earlier of the day the old mountain lion died."

"Yes, Otto, that day is burned into my mind."

"Remember the story I told you as we were riding together back to camp?"

Gray Owl parted his lips and smiled, and Otto again was reminded how handsome the Indian looked when he showed off his straight white teeth.

"As you face Bull, keep in mind that even though Goliath was bigger, David was clever and won the battle."

Gray Owl nodded. "I will take this story with me as I face Bull in battle."

Otto walked over to where Little Feather stood holding the reins of his pony just outside the corral. Victoria and Chandler joined Otto and the boy was comforted when Victoria silently cupped her hand inside his.

Five minutes later Gray Owl and Bull stood facing each other in the center of the corral. McAuliffe addressed the men. "This'll be a fair fight. No guns, knives, or clubs allowed. You will commence to fighting when I say go. It ends when one man says it ends or when one of you is knocked out. At that time, I expect you both to shake hands and we'll end it here. Do you understand?" Both men nodded their heads. Mac stepped outside the corral and shouted, "Go!"

The Indian had stripped to his loin cloth and the muscles on his legs and arms glistened with sweat in the late morning heat. He crouched low with his legs spread wide to maintain good balance and looked at his opponent.

Bull had removed his shirt and boots and slowly circled the corral with a grin spread across his face. The cowboy's thick neck supported a barrel chest and a slightly flabby stomach. Powerfully raised arms extended out from his chest and he looked like a bear ready to pounce on the Indian. Bull knew that if he could wrestle the Indian to the dirt, his weight advantage would give him an edge.

Bull lunged at Gray Owl but the Indian stepped to the side and he lost his balance and tumbled to the ground. He rolled over twice before coming to stop on a pile of horse manure. The trail hand wiped the dung from his chest and heard laughter as he struggled to his feet. The laughter made him angry. Bull charged full speed at his opponent. Gray Owl's eyes were locked on his foe, and he decided to use the speed of Bull's movement against him. At the last moment, the Indian gracefully stepped out of harm's way and pushed Bull onward by kicking him in the backside with his foot. The cowboy felt the sting of the wood against his head as he collided into the fence. The crash dazed him and for a moment he wondered where he was. He shook off the cloudy feeling in his head and began to circle the Indian. Bull needed to catch his breath and look for an advantage. He decided to taunt the Indian in hopes of aggravating him into making a charge.

"Face me and fight ya dirty redskin! Or else that pretty wife of yours will think yer a yellow-bellied chicken. Maybe she'd rather have a real man – like me."

Gray Owl could see Bull's mouth moving, but he could not hear the words that poured from his lips. He knew he was in a trance – the kind of trance that he had prayed to his ancestors for during the time he had been sent to the prairie as a young boy to complete his vision quest. Everything outside the corral had faded to a blur. All of his senses were focused on the movements of the man who had tormented him for so long. To Gray Owl, it was as though he knew every move the trail hand was going to make seconds before it happened and he readied himself to counter the attacks with the cunning of a mountain lion and the cleverness of David.

The cowboy charged once more, but his movements came slowly to Gray Owl's eyes – as though the trail hand was moving under water. As Bull lumbered toward Gray Owl, the Indian turned his body to spin sideways. His hand delivered a crushing blow to the base of Bull's head and the cowboy dropped to the dirt like a roped calf. Gray Owl stood over his adversary for a minute until the cheering sounds from the crowd gradually rushed toward him like the wind on the prairie. The cowboy was waking up and Gray Owl helped him to a sitting position. He reached out his hand to his opponent, but Bull slapped the hand aside and wiped away the dirt and manure from his eyes.

Gray Owl searched the crowd until he found his beloved Little Feather who was still standing next to Victoria and Otto. He walked toward the place where she stood near the edge of the fence.

Out of the corner of his eye, Otto saw Bull pull something from his pocket. He watched in confusion as the trail hand fiddled with the item. Suddenly, a flash of light reflected off its surface and Otto realized that the shine came from the metal blade of a pocket knife. With lightning speed, the enraged trail hand raised his arm and threw the knife at Gray Owl's back.

Otto yelled out to Gray Owl. Instinctively, the Indian dropped to a crouched position. Amid the chaos, Otto heard the sickening sound of a thud as the blade missed Gray Owl but hit something else. The horrified boy yelled out in terror as Victoria's hand slid away from his. Otto thought he might be sick as he looked down at his friend crumpled in the dirt with the sharp blade of a knife impaled in her chest.

Chapter 17 ~ August – The California Trail

Otto walked over to the Dickerson's camp at sunset to bring some wild flowers to his ailing friend who was recuperating inside the Dickerson's covered wagon. A week had passed since Victoria had clung to life after the knife had been removed from her chest.

Earlier in the evening, after they had rounded the wagons into a circle, McAuliffe gathered the members together to announce that they were camping at a place called Soda Springs, and in the morning the train would take the fork in the rode which pointed to the south and at long last become a part of the California Trail.

The captain addressed the group. "Despite the extra layover at Fort Bridger, we have made decent time getting this far west. The next portion of our journey will test your nerves and your patience. We'll follow the Humboldt River across a dry stretch of land, known as the Great Basin, 'til it peters out at a spot called Humboldt Sink. From there, you'll cross sixty-five miles of desert with no grass for the oxen, and the brackish watering holes that you'll find along the way will be few and far between. We'll carry what extra water we can manage across the barren desert until the trail drops us at the foot of the Sierra Nevada Mountain Range. You'll be painfully tired at this point, but there'll be no time to lollygag around. The mountain trails of the Sierras are well marked, but it will be vital to make good time as we pull the wagons up the steep slopes. We don't want to get caught up on top and face the possibility of an early snow. We all know what happened to the Donner Party back in forty-six."

Otto saw genuine concern in the faces of the pioneers who stood closest to him. He decided that he would not pass this information on to Victoria. It would be pointless to worry her in her guarded condition.

The knife wound had punctured Victoria's right lung and the girl had struggled to breathe for twelve hours under the care of a local doctor who lived at Fort Bridger. The doctor instinctively wanted to boot Otto out of his office, but the boy had insisted on staying at the side of his friend, all the while trickling water onto her lips from a fancy purple bottle he held in his hands. The parents of the girl agreed that the boy should be allowed to stay and do whatever he felt necessary with his bottle. But the doctor insisted that it would not be decent for Otto to stay through the delicate surgery. Otto offered to leave only if the doctor would swear to treat Victoria's wound with water from the bottle. The doctor looked at the girl's parents who were vigorously nodding their heads, threw up his hand, and agreed to the promise.

After the doctor had removed the knife and dressed the wound, Otto came and stayed at Victoria's side all through the night ministering to her with the water from the bottle. Incredibly, the young girl made remarkable improvement from a puncture wound that could have easily been fatal.

McAuliffe held up the train for two extra days until he felt certain that Victoria was stable enough to travel with the members. Bull had been thrown into Bridger's stockade. Jim assured Mac that the trail hand would stay put until army soldiers could escort the scoundrel back to Fort Laramie where he would serve time for attempted murder.

Victoria smiled at Otto as he placed the yellow and purple flowers into her hands and said, "They're beautiful, Otto."

Otto's face reddened as he answered, "I never before found any like these on the prairie. And…well, I wanted you to see them first. Otto shifted on the stool he had pulled close to her bunk and asked, "Will you be allowed to walk around soon?"

"I think so. I'm tired of jostling about inside this prairie schooner. My folks are going to let me walk beside the wagon for a little while tomorrow during the day. I feel so much better and wish you'd take back your beautiful Amethyst Bottle. It seems that I've had it more than you on this wagon train."

"You must keep the bottle a few more days. Then, I will take it back."

"Thank you, Otto."

"What is to thank me for?"

"Ma told me what you did with the bottle. I don't remember much of anything during that time, but I'm happy that you were there with me."

"It was nothing."

"How's Gray Owl? He comes by the wagon everyday with Little Feather. The look on his face is so sad. I tell him that it's not his fault, but I don't know if he believes me."

"Gray Owl has spoken of this with Captain McAuliffe and me many times these past days. We told him that he was just reacting to my warning-call about the knife. I'm as much to blame as anyone."

"Otto, no one is to blame. I'm just happy that Bull is locked up. I would feel worried if he were roaming free. There was always something about him that made me quiver."

"Quiver? What is this new word, quiver?"

Victoria smiled, "It means to tremble or shake in a nervous way."

"Well then, I will quiver until you are well enough to go for walks with me and we can discuss the latest book you gave to me."

Victoria looked fondly at Otto and laughed.

The wagon train had been traveling along the Humboldt River for three days. Otto wondered why McAuliffe had sent Gray Owl to fetch him from his morning duty saddling the horses for the day's ride. He felt nervous as he walked the horses over to the campfire wondering if he had done something to displease his boss. Otto saw the captain smoking a cigarette and drinking a cup of coffee as Biscuit cleared away the remnants of breakfast. Biscuit smiled at Otto and handed him a plate filled with bacon, biscuits, and beans. Kirby, Little Feather and Gray Owl sat quietly around the breakfast campfire looking very somber.

"There's coffee in the pot, Otto. Pour yerself a cup," commanded the cook.

"Thanks, Biscuit."

"Sit down, Otto," offered McAuliffe.

Otto grabbed a camp stool and plunked down next to the captain. "Is everything alright, Captain? Is there problem with my work?"

Captain McAuliffe laughed until the bellowing sound turned into a hacking cough. He looked at his cigarette and threw it into the campfire. "Is that why you think I sent for you, Otto?"

"I did not know."

"It's rather the opposite. You've been a big help to me, Otto. You pulled your share of the load and that's what I want to talk to you about. You know that we're short a man with Bull being arrested for attempted murder."

"This I know."

"I was wondering if I might call on you to take over some of his duties like guarding the camp at night. I'm pulling in some of the members to take a turn. You see, we're in an area inhabited by the Ute Indians. They're a lot like the Crows in that they're fond of stealing horses. I want to double up on the guards at night. I sure could use an extra hand, and there'd be a bonus in it for you at the end of the trail."

Otto sat up at little straighter in his stool and let out a sigh of relief. "I would be most honored to take on this extra duty for you, Captain."

"Good. That's exactly what I was hoping to hear." The captain reached around behind him and dragged out a gunny sack, which he placed on the ground between Otto and himself. "There are some things in here that belonged to Bull. Since he won't have much need for them at Fort Laramie, I've decided to give them to you. Go on and open it up."

Otto placed the food and coffee, which he had not touched, on the ground and carefully opened the sack. Inside he found a gun and holster, a large Bowie Knife in its sheath, designed by the legendary frontiersman Jim Bowie, and a half-dozen boxes filled with bullets. Otto looked at McAuliffe, but was speechless.

"I can't send you out at night to guard the camp unarmed, Otto, so I thought it best to make you a gift of Bull's things. Reckon he owed you that much."

"But, Captain, I do not know how to shoot."

Mac laughed. You're always thinking ahead aren't you, Otto."

"Yes, I try to think with my head, Captain."

The trail boss chuckled and said, "Well don't worry. I'm going to ride out with you later today and give you your first lesson. Do you know what kind of gun this is?'

"No, Sir."

"Well, Bull prided himself on owning the best equipment when it came to weaponry. This gun, Otto, is a Colt revolver. Samuel Colt invented the pistol and got a patent on it in 1836. Now, a lot of other men tried to make revolvers, but his was the first real successful model."

Otto listened in fascination as McAuliffe told him about the history of the gun called the revolver. He became reminded again at how much the trail boss knew about so many things and how much he wanted to become like him.

"Now look here, Otto." Mac picked up the gun and removed it from its holster. He opened the barrel and made certain that there were no bullets in the chambers. Otto watched as he rotated the cylinder. "The revolver has a cylinder with six firing chambers in it." McAuliffe pulled back on the hammer of the pistol with his thumb. "Each time the hammer is cocked or the trigger is pulled the cylinder revolves and places a new bullet in direct line with the barrel. A man can fire off six shots before he has to reload. But that's not all that's remarkable about a Colt revolver. The gun is rugged. You can drop it in the sand or on a rock and most times it'll be alright. I've even seen one trampled by a horse and the darn thing still worked. The sight is a bit off, but I'll teach you all about that later. I've got to get this train moving in a few minutes, but I want you to think about what I'm going to say before we take our first lesson, Otto"

"I will."

"A gun can be a good weapon for defense against hostile Indians, animals or an enemy, but you should only use it as a last measure. Wearing a gun brings with it a big responsibility.

It's not for a kid, and that's why I'm giving it to you, Otto. I consider you to be one of my men. Do you understand?"

Otto nodded his head and said, "I understand, Captain. I will not disappoint you."

"Good. But for now, you better eat up Biscuit's grub. Then put this sack under your bunk in the wagon." McAuliffe looked at the group sitting around the dying embers of the campfire and announced, "Step lively, men. Let's get this wagon train rolling."

Otto and Captain McAuliffe found a small dried ravine that Mac thought would be a good place to practice with the gun. The two had ridden out a mile from the wagon train at the start of the nooning meal. McAuliffe removed the weapon from its sack and adjusted the holster to Otto's hip.

"The belt's a might too large for you, Otto. Guess Bull was a stretch bigger around the middle. I'll ask Isaac Wise if he can tailor the belt to fit you. It's not important for you to wear it for your first lesson today."

Otto removed the holster from his hip, and Cornelius placed it back in the sack. McAuliffe set the revolver on a rock next to a box of bullets. He reached into the sack and pulled a large Bowie knife. He removed it from its sheath and let Otto hold it. "What do you think?'

"It is very striking, Captain." Otto was surprised at the weight of the knife. The blade was about nine inches long with the end curving into a razor sharp tip. An ivory handle was set into a metal frame which had a T-shaped crosspiece that separated the handle from the polished blade. Otto's hand trembled with the thought of ever having to use the imposing weapon in self-defense.

McAuliffe could sense that Otto was a bit nervous holding the knife. "History tells us that sometime around 1825, James Bowie lost his grip and cut his hand on the blade of the knife he was using at the time. The legendary frontier hero decided that a metal guard, called a bolster was needed to keep his hand from slipping onto the blade. It is said that Bowie had the blade and handle so well balanced that he could throw it with a great deal of accuracy."

"Is James Bowie alive today?'

"No, Otto. Jim Bowie died on March 6, 1836, along with about two hundred other brave men who were defending a fort in Texas called the Alamo. The knife's yours, Otto. Treat it with respect and it'll prove to be useful for many things."

Otto looked at the knife and frowned He remembered seeing the imposing weapon worn around Bull's waist.

"What's the matter, Otto?"

"I was just thinking Captain. I hope I never have to use this knife in battle."

"That's something that the majority of men feel as well. Still, it's important to know *how* to use it...just in case. But, for today, we'll concentrate on using the pistol for target practice."

Otto watched Mac walk out about twenty yards. The captain searched the area until he found five rocks, equal in size to an medium-sized pinecone. He spaced them apart on the ledge of a large round bolder which Otto thought to be around five feet high. Cornelius walked back to where Otto was nervously standing and showed Otto how to load the gun. "This raised bit on the front of the gun is called a *sight*. Use you your eyes to line up the sight with the rock you want to hit. A greenhorn might try closing one eye, but a good marksman knows to keep both eyes open. Would you like me to show you?"

"Yes, please."

Otto watched as McAuliffe lined up the sight of the gun with the target and fired off one shot. The rock on the far left flew into the air and landed in the dirt ten feet away. Otto let out the air he was holding in his lungs and nodded his head in admiration.

"Now you try."

Otto's hand shook, but he willed himself to steady his nerves. He held the gun straight out and pointed it toward the remaining four rocks. McAuliffe showed him how to stand and where to look with the sight. Otto squeezed the trigger and the rock on the far right leapt into the air.

"That's amazing, Otto. You hit your mark on the very first try!"

Otto looked sheepishly at the wagon master and shrugged his shoulders. "Well, not exactly, Captain. I was aiming for the rock next to the one you hit."

Chapter 18 ~ August 1854 – Humboldt Sink

Captain McAuliffe sent Kirby and Otto on horseback around the circled wagons to alert the members that Gray Owl had seen signs that Indians were in the territory and to take extra precautions with their belongings. His orders were to pack away all provisions and belongings inside the wagons but not to panic. A contingent of armed men would be posted around the perimeter of the wagon train for added protection. The day before, McAuliffe had informed the pioneers that they would spend an extra day at Humboldt Sink to prepare for the long trek across the desert. Extra grass, hay and water for the animals had been collected in anticipation of the grueling sixty-mile journey through a barren desert known as the Carson Trail, which would take them to the base of the Sierra Nevada Mountain Range.

"Whoa, Hawkeye!" commanded Otto. The boy adjusted his backside to the seat on the saddle and surveyed the Dickerson's camp. He saw Chandler and waved to him.

Chandler looked up from his place near the campfire and waved back at Otto. He admired his Russian friend who looked all grown up sitting astride his painted pony wearing a new gun and holster on his right hip and a large Bowie knife strapped in its sheath on the left side of his waist.

Otto greeted Julia Dickerson who was busy putting away the remnants of the evening meal. He noticed Isaac Wise talking to Tony Dickerson near the back of the wagon. The men waved and walked over to where Otto was seated on his pony.

Isaac beamed at Otto and said, "I am happy to see that the belt on your holster is now properly fitted to your waist. I left plenty of room on the belt for growing."

"Thank you, Mr. Wise," answered Otto as he looked down at the belt attached to the holster. "It is indeed a perfect fit."

"It was my pleasure to fix it for you Otto," the cobbler gushed.

Tony Dickerson looked up at Otto and spoke. "I think I know why you're here, Otto. The captain stopped by earlier and asked me to share an eight hour shift with Isaac tonight. He'll stand guard the first four hours and wake me up around midnight."

Otto smiled at Victoria who had stepped down from the wagon and was walking toward the group. He waved and then turned his attention back to Tony. "The captain says the wagon train will most likely be alright, but it is best to be prepared."

Julia walked over and handed Otto a bundle of calico cloth tied at the top. "Here are a couple of hunks of cornbread left over from dinner. Thought ya might like to gnaw on these later, Otto, if'n ya get hungry."

"Thank you, Mrs. Dickerson."

Before turning to leave, Otto waved to the younger girls, Jessica and Christina, who were playing a game with Chandler near the wagon.

"Take care tonight, Otto," cautioned Victoria.

Otto cleared his throat and said, "I will be most careful, Victoria." He tipped his hat to the group and urged his horse to the next camp.

As Otto rode away, he thought how completely healthy his friend looked. She could walk for hours without tiring. Victoria and Otto had not resumed their walks during the afternoons, because Otto was busy with the extra duties he had taken on for the captain. Otto made an effort to stop by the Dickerson's camp each evening to check on her. They would spend some time reading poetry or just talking about stories they had heard about California and the rush to find gold.

Sir Nigel Churchstone and Simon Walton were busy preparing their beautifully equipped wagon for the long trek across the desert. "Good evening, young Otto," said Simon as he tightened a water barrel to the side of the wagon with rope. Sir Nigel wiped the sweat from his brow with a spotlessly white handkerchief.

"Good evening," greeted Otto.

Sir Nigel looked at the boy and thought how much Otto had changed from the young lad whom he had first come to meet in Elm Grove at the start of the journey. He smiled inwardly thinking of the shy nervous boy who was anxiously trying to please his boss. "By Jove, Otto, you look like a veteran cowboy sitting astride your horse all kitted out with your pistol and holster. You've grown like prairie grass these past months. What brings you to our modest little encampment tonight?"

"Captain McAuliffe wanted me to warn you that Gray Owl has seen signs of Indians, most likely Utes, in the area. He is posting extra guards tonight just to be safe. He wants everyone to store their goods in the wagons and not stray too far from the area to do any…well…personal business with nature."

Nigel laughed out loud and said, "Simon and I shall use our chamber pot if the need arises throughout the night. Thank you for the warning about the Indians. Does the captain need any more men to help with the watch?"

"The captain posted the sign for the men who are on duty tonight and you are not on the list this time. Just keep your ears open for any suspicious sounds. We'll break camp before sun-up to get a start on the trip across the desert."

"Right then. Good luck, lad, and do be extra careful tonight."

Otto touched the brim of his hat, and said good night. The young boy reflected on how much he liked the two Englishmen as he guided Hawkeye to the next camp.

Otto's chin fell forward onto his chest. The movement caused him to jerk his head up, and he momentarily wondered where he was until Hawkeye tramped sideways. "Steady, boy." The faint light from a half moon spilled onto the circled wagons and Otto remembered that he was standing guard duty for Captain McAuliffe. He pulled the Amethyst Bottle from its case, pulled the stopper off the top, and let the cool liquid trickle into his mouth. Otto splashed some water down the back of his neck and down the front of his shirt in an effort to refresh his tired body. The night was sticky and hot. Otto thought it would have been easier to stay awake if there were a chill in the air, but the warm summer breeze wrapped around his body like a saddle blanket tempting him to doze off when he knew he should be alert.

Just at that moment a flash of lightening sparked in the distance and Otto could momentarily see a smattering of scrub brush dotting the northern horizon. Otto counted. One. . .two. . .three. . .four. Thunder crashed and Otto knew that the storm was about four miles to the south. *If this **hullabaloo** keeps up,* he thought, *I may never sleep tonight.* He smiled at the new word he had learned from Chandler that meant loud noises. Otto loosened the calico sack that he had attached to his saddle horn and nudged Hawkeye into a walk with the heels of his boots. *If I* *keep moving and eat Mrs. Dickerson's cornbread, I will not be as tempted to close my eyes.*

Otto urged Hawkeye onward. He rode just outside the circle of wagons and looked in between the gaps to make certain no one was lurking in the shadows. He had just finished the first piece of the cornbread when he passed Kirby who was riding his horse in the opposite direction.

"Hello Kirby. Would you like a piece of Mrs. Dickerson's cornbread?"

Kirby smiled as he took the offering into his hand. "Thanks, Otto. Mrs. Dickerson makes a fine skillet of cornbread."

"What time do you make it to be, Kirby?"

Kirby pulled his watch from the pocket of his suede vest and opened the cover. "It's just after midnight. I reckon the captain will be by in an hour to take over my watch. I feel like I could sleep for three days, but with that storm approaching who knows. Who's relieving you?"

"Jonas Martin."

"He's a good man. Keep your eyes peeled 'til he arrives." Kirby urged his horse onward.

Otto glanced down at his new knife and gun securely strapped to his waist. He had continued his shooting lessons with McAuliffe and Gray Owl, who was an expert with knives, but still felt uneasy wearing the weapons. Otto kept them tucked safely under his bunk when he was attending to his jobs during the day, and only wore them when he ventured away from camp or when he was on guard duty at night.

The tired boy pulled Hawkeye to a stop. He eased the Amethyst Bottle from its case and spilled some of the last of the water into his open mouth. He put the stopper back in place and looked at the beautiful bottle that seemed to glimmer even in the dimness of the night. Otto thought of his brother Ivan. *I wonder, Ivan, if you wear a gun and ride a horse. I wonder if we will happen to know each other's faces if we are fortunate enough to meet up in San Francisco. I think you may not recognize me.*

A crunching sound nearby gave Otto a jolt. Otto tugged on the reins of his horse, and Hawkeye responded by standing still. "Steady boy."

Suddenly the hairs on the back of Otto's neck stood up and a sudden chill washed over his skin. Out of the corner of his eye, Otto saw a brief scurrying behind one of the scraggly bushes that dotted the nearly barren landscape. He wondered if it might be coyotes lured into camp by the smell of livestock. Slowly, Otto shifted the bottle to his left hand and pulled the Colt revolver from his holster and gently rested it on his thigh, while pointing it in the general direction of the movement.

Cold sweat formed on Otto's brow. His mouth went dry and the rhythm of his heart seemed to beat as fast as the wings on a hummingbird. Otto looked up and down the perimeter of the wagon train hoping to see Kirby or Gray Owl, but for the moment, he seemed to be all alone. Straining his eyes, Otto peered through the half light of the moon hoping to see a coyote or even a mountain lion behind the bush. Otto tied the reins of the horse to his saddle horn and wrestled with his left hand to lift the leather case to his chest so that he might slip the Amethyst Bottle safely back into its satchel.

At that moment, another flash of lightning illuminated the sky. Otto gasped to see three Indians, crouching behind a small outcropping of bushes, staring back at him. Fierce looking paint covered their faces, but something looked vaguely out of place to Otto. For an instant, he could have sworn that one of the braves looked like Bull, but Otto knew that Bull had been taken to Fort Laramie to serve time for stabbing Victoria. Otto dismissed the thought knowing he had to use his wits to concentrate on what he should do. He wanted to peel off a warning shot in the air to alert the other guards, but he could not will himself to pick up the gun from his lap. Instead, he sat frozen in his saddle with fear.

In the next second, an arrow shot through the air and landed near his chest. The arrowhead might well have entered Otto's heart had it not been for the Amethyst Bottle that he had just slipped into its case. Instead the arrow ricocheted off the case and bounced unceremoniously in the dirt. Before Otto had time to think, a second arrow whizzed past his ear ending up in a wooden barrel attached to the side of a wagon.

The brush with the two arrows nudged Otto into action. Without giving much thought to his next move, Otto lifted the gun from his lap and fired the pistol in the direction of the brush. A yelp from one of the men penetrated the night air. Otto listened to the frantic sounds of the intruders talking in garbled tones he did not understand. The men seemed panicky and in an instant Otto heard the soft pounding of footsteps retreating away into the night.

After that everything blended into a blur of activity. Men were rushing toward him from every direction with a thousand questions, which Otto found impossible to answer.

Finally, Captain McAuliffe appeared from nowhere and silenced the frantic mob with a loud whistle. "I need all of you men to go back to your posts. There may be more trouble on the horizon and we'll need a strong perimeter defense. Gray Owl, you and Kirby stay here with me." The men realized the wisdom in McAuliffe's words and immediately returned to their stations.

Mac looked passed Otto and noticed the arrow stuck in the barrel. Gray Owl picked the other arrow up from the dirt and looked puzzled when he saw that the tip had shattered into many small pieces. He showed the arrow to McAuliffe who whistled softly in bewilderment.

Otto looked on in dazed confusion as Mac motioned for Kirby and Gray Owl to search the area leading away from the path of the arrow in the bucket. He stared at Otto who was still gripping the Colt with his right hand and clutching the case of the Amethyst Bottle in the other hand and said, "Otto, put your gun back in its holster." Otto's hand shook as he slipped the gun into its leather casing. "Can you tell me what happened?"

Otto pointed in the direction of the bushes and uttered in gasping tones, "There…three. . .three Indians with paint on their faces crouching in the bushes. I saw them as the lightning flashed in the sky. I may have injured one. I heard someone cry out, and then I heard footsteps. I think they ran away."

"Are you alright?"

Otto rubbed the area where, in all likelihood, the arrow should have entered his chest. "I think so. One of the arrows came straight for my chest, but I think it hit my bottle instead."

"Are you sure you're not hit?"

"My bottle!" Otto quickly pulled the bottle from its case and inspected the glass. He scoured the surface with his hands looking for chips or cracks and let out a breath of air from his lungs when it appeared that the bottle was in perfect condition. The arrowhead had penetrated the leather casing, and Otto reached inside the leather pouch and stuck his finger through the hole. "

McAuliffe looked at the pretty bottle in Otto's hands. "You seem mighty partial to that bottle, Otto. I must admit it is quite striking. The color reminds me of something." The captain seemed lost in thought before he added, "I just can't remember what it is. You say the first arrow hit the bottle?"

"Yes, I am certain of it." Otto held up the leather pouch and wiggled his finger through a hole.

Cornelius showed Otto the smashed pieces of the tip of the arrowhead that had been fashioned from a shiny black rock known as obsidian. "That certainly is some interesting bottle you've got there Otto. It was strong enough to stop this arrowhead from piercing your chest. But we'll talk more about that later. Are you sure you're alright?"

Otto tore his eyes away from the shattered pieces of obsidian resting in the captain's hands and answered, "Yes, but Captain, I feel very confused. When the lightning lit up the sky, I think I see that one of the Indians looked very much like Bull." Otto shivered again. "I guess my mind was playing tricks on me. It all happened so fast."

"If anyone's still out there, Kirby and Gray Owl will track 'em down. Let's you and I head back to the camp. You need to try and get some sleep. We have a big day heading across the desert tomorrow."

Otto looked at the man whom he admired so much and nodded his head. He questioned how one minute he could be so tired and now feel so very wide awake. He wondered if sleep would come.

Kirby and Gray Owl returned to the wagon train a few hours later. McAuliffe had ordered Otto to his bunk after the attack. He stayed with the boy until he had finally fallen to sleep. McAuliffe had just finished making his rounds for the second time and had returned to camp after the men who guarded the circle of wagons reported to him that all was quiet. He breathed a sigh of relief that the incident seemed to be an isolated attack by a few rogue Indians.

Mac nodded to his valued workers as he wearily removed the saddle from Dickens' back. The grumpy horse nipped at McAuliffe's sleeve as he placed a bucket of water on the ground. The captain knew that the tired horse was as much on edge as he was with his sleep having been interrupted with the raid. McAuliffe tied the horse's halter to the wheel of the wagon and patted him on the rump. "Try and get some sleep, my friend. You'll have a long day of work ahead of you."

Cornelius looked at his trusted men and asked, "What'd ya find?"

Gray Owl explained, "We find foot tracks leading to three horses tied to some bushes. There is much fresh blood in sand near where men walk to get horses. We follow horse tracks for some time, but riders fly like the wind to the north."

Kirby broke in to add his thoughts. "We figured it'd be best if we didn't venture too far away from the train. Besides, it looks like it was probably a few renegade braves lookin' to steal some horses or rifles. I think Otto probably winged one with his gun and they tried to hightail it outta here to patch the bullet wound before the injured one bled to death."

McAuliffe nodded his head in agreement. "It'll be light in a few hours. You two head off to sleep. We have a long day ahead of us."

Kirby looked at the captain and asked, "What about you? You look done in."

"I think I'll just stoke up this fire and rest here. Biscuit will be up before long and he'll keep me company."

Gray Owl looked at the man who had once saved him from certain death. He watched as the captain started to roll a cigarette, but changed his mind. From the edge of the campfire the Indian saw how tired he looked.

Left alone with his thoughts, McAuliffe stared at the small pouch of tobacco that he used to role his cigarettes and wondered if the tobacco had been at the root of his illness. Deep in his heart, he knew he should not be smoking. Last spring in New York Doc Simpson had verified what he had suspected for some time. An examination confirmed that his lungs may have been compromised due to his many years as a smoker. The sympathetic doctor had told him that he had seen cases like this before and that there was little that could be done for him. The doctor suggested that Cornelius stop smoking immediately.

"How much time do you reckon I have Doc Simpson?"

Simpson shook his head. "It's not certain how much time you have. It could be six months. It could be three years. We don't know enough about this illness. You might want to go home and spend time with your family."

McAuliffe had smiled at the doctor. I have a friend in San Francisco. I'll take the wagon train west and retire there. It's a good place to settle down."

Cornelius knew that he was not the type to sit around and wait to die or to burden his family with his troubles, so he finished buying his supplies and hired the scrappy new wrangler named Otto to join his wagon train. Mac had known that the trip out west would be his last journey to California. He told no one of his illness, but made a specification in writing, that if his failing health would not allow him to lead his members, he would turn the outfit over to Kirby and Gray Owl. Mac knew Kirby would find where the captain kept his important papers. He had no regrets and reckoned it would be best to keep busy and let life's trail take him where it would. He had notified his bank in California with specific instructions, that in the event of his passing, to leave half of his life's savings to Kirby and the other half to Gray Owl. He had directed the bank to provide Biscuit with an extra cash bonus for his many years of service to his outfit. At fort Bridger, he had left instructions to amended his will to include another cash bonus for Otto in recognition of the extra duty he had taken on after Bull had been arrested.

Mac looked westward and let out a long sigh. He tossed his unfinished cigarette into the fire and closed his eyes. The wagon master harbored no regrets, but he prayed that he would remain healthy enough to finish the job of leading his members safely to San Francisco. He knew that if he made it to California, he would not be leaving the shores of the Pacific Ocean again.

Chapter 19 ~ September 1854 –
Truckee River Camp

Otto could not remember when he had ever been happier. The wagon train had successfully crossed the harsh dessert by way of the Carson Trail and was camping on the eastern side of the High Sierras below the summit of Donner Pass. Spirits were high, knowing, once they tamed the steep hurdle of Donner Pass, all that was left was a moderate decent down the mountain into the Sacramento Valley.

Earlier in the day, Gray Owl and Otto had ridden over to a meadow where the Donner Party had camped back in 1847. Otto was astonished to see a grove of trees that had been sawn off eighteen feet high from the ground. Gray Owl told him that the height marked where the snow line had grown to throughout the harsh winter. In final desperation, the forlorn group had sawed the treetops off for firewood. Not a branch remained on the sides of the trunks and the trees looked like an odd formation of poles. Otto said a silent prayer for all of the pioneers who had given up so much to travel west to California.

The newly formed state, known as California, had joined the union as the thirty-first state in 1850. Buoyed by the success of the Mexican-American War, the United States had claimed vast areas of land in an 1848 treaty with Mexico, which included California, Arizona, New Mexico and Nevada. The discovery of gold in 1849 tempted thousands of people from all over the world to come to California to seek their fortune in the gold fields known as the mother-lode region. Others were pulled to the territory by newspaper articles touting valleys with lush soil and mild winters. The new settlers sought to claim land for farming and ranching away from the vast Mexican ranchos that once dominated the land. By most accounts, California was judged to be a booming success.

Otto sat near the edge of the Truckee River looking down at his journal, and reread his account of the past month to his mother.

Tuesday, 19 of September

Dear Mama,

As organized as we were, the trip across the desert took our group by surprise. Our members had been warned that the journey through the hot barren land would be hard, but I know they were not prepared for the toll it would take on their minds and their bodies. Without the expert guidance of Captain McAuliffe, I am certain we may have perished along with the graveyard of wagons and animal skeletons that lay scattered across the desert floor like cast off chicken bones.

Before sunrise, the captain would sound the call to wake the weary travelers. He knew it was important to travel when the air was cooler and the sun less angry. At breakfast, the captain would instruct Kirby, Grey Owl, and me to pass among the wagons. We reminded the members to ration their water and grass to the livestock. Throughout the day, we encouraged them to keep up their spirits as we moved forward. The captain made the group rest during the hottest hours of the day under the shelter of blankets and tarps so they would be fit enough to continue their march in the late afternoon when the air became slightly cooler. It took the train a week to cross the sandy terrain. Sometimes the going was easy. At other times, the wagon wheels would be buried half way up in sand and the poor oxen would strain with the effort to move onward.

No one bothered to use their precious water for bathing and by the second day, the pioneers looked almost ghost-like from the alkaline dust and sand which stuck to their hair and clothes and crept into their eyes and up their noses. During this time I saw little of my friend, Victoria and the Dickerson family as our group trudged further into the desert. The old camp routine of the evenings, which had been common all summer, seemed like a far-off dream. The members ate in weary silence and then staggered off to their beds with little talking. Each step took great effort and we knew it was important to save every ounce of strength so we could rise once more in darkness to the sound of the captain's horn and make our way across the scorched earth.

Our eyes remained fixed to the west. The sight of the Sierra Nevada Mountain Range willed our legs to move ahead toward the jagged green mountains, which grew ever larger with each passing day. To our weary eyes, the mountains signified the cooling shade of trees

and icy mountain water from lakes and streams
– water that could replenish our spirits and
nourish our bodies.

Your loving son, Otto

Suddenly, Otto heard Biscuit's voice calling him to dinner and instinctively his stomach began to growl. He tucked the journal under his armpit and trotted toward the smell of food.

Otto handed his empty plate to Biscuit. "Gee, Otto, it'll be an easy job cleanin' this plate. There's nothin' but bones on it. Ain't one bite of fish or crumb of biscuit left behind, and that's a complement to the cook! By the looks of them pants up over yer ankles, you'd best be usin' some of your wages to buy a pair of them new sturdy prospecting pants, that Isaac Wise was tellin' us about, when we reach San Francisco. You've been growin' like a stalk of corn all summer long."

Otto glanced down at his pants and noticed that they barely covered his boots. "It is your fault, Biscuit. You feed me too well. Your fried fish was most delicious tonight. My stomach is full."

"You can thank Little Feather in part. She certainly has a gift for catchin' fish. She has also introduced me to some plants in the forest that I never would've tried on my own. They sort of liven up the flavors a bit."

Otto glanced over to where Little Feature sat next to Gray Owl. He smiled at her and thought she looked more beautiful than ever. Together, they made a handsome couple. Gray Owl appeared to smile all the time these days. It was wonderful for Otto to see his friend so happy.

The young boy frowned slightly when he turned his head toward Captain McAuliffe. The captain had grown increasingly thin over the course of their trek out west and Otto thought that his boss's skin looked dull and seemed marked with tones of gray and yellow. He also noticed that the captain had given up smoking his tobacco and that his cough seemed to have eased a bit. A sudden chill began to emanate from the bottle at Otto's side. The chilling sensation quickly spread through the boy's body causing him to shudder.

A few days ago, Otto had stumbled across his boss as he lay resting against the trunk of a tree at twilight. He had been invited to join the captain and they talked of many things, including the captain's failing health. At length, Otto offered to loan the Amethyst Bottle to Mac, as he had once done for Victoria.

Otto recalled how Cornelius had gathered the bottle into his hands and stared at it in quiet contemplation for a few minutes. "This bottle has an alluring quality attached to it. I witnessed first hand what good it did for your friend, Victoria." McAuliffe stroked the base of the bottle and found the raised edges of the Latin poem inscribed at its base. He pulled a wooden match from his vest pocket and struck the tip against a nearby rock. Holding the flame near the bottle's base, he easily translated the words from Latin to English.

Into thy hands I come.
Unto thy spirit as one.

Otto gasped in astonishment and said, "I did not know that you could speak Latin. In truth, Latin is a language that I too would like to study."

McAuliffe looked at the boy and began to chuckle. "You seem to pick up languages with the ease of someone collecting stones, Otto, so I have no doubt that you could easily master Latin as well."

Otto's spirits lifted with the words of praise from his boss. "If I am not being too bold, Captain, might I ask where you learned Latin?"

McAuliffe looked off into the distance and began speaking, "When I was a young man of twenty, my parents sent me to a fine military school called West Point in New York. My fellow cadets and I were not only taught the strategies of war so that we might one day become first-rate officers, we were also instructed in history, math, language, art, and literature so that we might also become first-rate gentlemen."

"What you say, explains a lot to me about your character, Captain."

Cornelius looked at the surface of the bottle again and said, "Remember that I once told you that the color of this bottle reminded me of something, but I couldn't recall what?"

"I remember the time well. It was the night the Ute Indians invaded our camp. It was this very bottle that protected my chest from the tip of an arrowhead."

"That's right. I just now came to realize that this color brings a memory to me so vivid, it's like it happened yesterday."

Otto listened in fascination as McAuliffe shared his story.

"During my years at West Point, dances were sometimes given with invitations sent out to young society ladies from all over New York. I remember spending one particularly enjoyable evening in the company of the daughter of a congressman from Albany. She was charming and a most accomplished dancer. I recall how this delicate violet silk scarf had been attached to her wrist with an interesting knot. The scarf floated in the air with each turn of our waltzes. After an evening of laughter and music, she awarded me with her violet-colored scarf at a token of her enjoyment of our time spent together, Even now, I recall how I felt like a Greek athlete receiving a laurel wreath for winning a race.

"I was in high spirits as I walked with my fellow cadets back to our barracks with the afore-mentioned scarf tucked jauntily into the waist of my crisp white dress pants and stone gray jacket. From out of the darkness of night, we became startled at the barking sound of a deep voice calling out, *'Attention cadets!'* I caught my breath as we quickly froze to attention.

"To my utter dismay, our supreme superintendent, Colonel Sylvanus Thayer stepped into view, walked straight up to me, and bellowed, *'You're out of uniform, soldier!'* Colonel Thayer removed the offending scarf from my waist and asked, *'What is the motto at West Point?'* To which we all promptly replied, *'Duty, Honor, Country, Sir!'* The colonel looked directly into my eyes and after what seemed an eternity, he uttered, *'Carry on then!'* And with that, Otto, we quickly scurried to our quarters in total silence."

McAuliffe chuckled softly and added, "I never laid eyes on the offending scarf again until I saw it attached to Mrs. Thayer's wrist at my graduation." It was then that I realized that Colonel Thayer had a unique sense of humor."

Otto asked, "What happened to your dance partner?"

McAuliffe chortled, "She married a banking tycoon. I heard she grew stout after giving her husband lots of children."

"Captain. The bottle helped my friend, Victoria. Take it. I'm sure it will help you!"

Mac handed the Amethyst Bottle back to Otto and said, "Thanks for offering me the bottle, Otto. I know what you're trying to do. Honestly speaking, holding your pretty bottle these past moments gives me the strength to think I might have been given some extra time to enjoy life in San Francisco after all."

Otto started to protest, but was cut off with the reflective words of the captain. "You see the truth is, Otto, this is my last trip as a wagon master. I'm tired. I have no regrets about my life. If I had one wish though, I think I would have never taken up smoking, I don't think tobacco is good for the body. But who knows. I've enjoyed bringing so many people safely out west. But now, I think I'll be happy to live out my days fishing and watching the sun set over the Pacific Ocean."

Otto shifted his thoughts to the present. *I will find ways to get the captain to hold the bottle, no matter what he says.* He suddenly realized that he had been staring at his trail boss. Otto blushed with embarrassment. It was as though the captain knew what Otto had been thinking because he smiled and gave Otto a nod.

McAuliffe broke the silence of the moment by directing a question to Otto which swayed the boy form his thoughts. "We'll be in San Francisco in a few weeks. Do you have a plan, Otto, to find your brother?"

"I have a plan, Captain. I think I will begin my search in the city by asking if anyone has heard of or seen a man with a Russian accent named Ivan Stanoff. Even if Ivan is in the gold fields, he may have met someone who would remember him." Otto let out a long slow breath and added, "I do not know, though. It has been over three years since I have had contact with him. It is a long time. It is my hope that he has been in communication with my mother, and she has told him of my trip west to find him from the letter Doc Simpson mailed for me in New York." Otto looked at the captain and shrugged.

"Three years *is* a long time, Otto, but California has a way of getting a hold on a man. It's not just the gold either. The climate is mild and the soil is rich – perfect conditions for growing crops and feeding all the people coming from every part of the globe to seek their fortune. It could be that Ivan may still be in the gold fields, or that he's started a business, or is farming. Things are booming all over California."

Otto was cheered with the thought he might truly find Ivan in California. He looked at the Cornelius and said, "I love the sound of the name California. What does it mean, Captain?" Mac cleared his throat, and said, "I love your desire, Otto, to want to learn about everything new to you. Asking about things is a good trait. Truth is, a few years back, I had dinner with a prominent ranchero and member of San Francisco society and asked him that same question. My friend, Señor De Lucien, shared a fascinating story with me that will answer your question.

"He told me that an early Spanish explorer, sailing off the coast of Baja California in the fifteen-hundreds, mistakenly thought that the peninsula was an island, so he named the land after a popular Spanish book from that time. The fictional story told of a mythical island filled with vast quantities of gold. The island was home to strong warrior women and their queen, Calafia, who ruled over them. No men were allowed on the island and large creatures called griffins, which had the head and wings of an eagle and the body and tail of a lion, protected the island from any invaders." Mac laughed and added, "Perhaps the warrior women were right to keep the men out. Historically, we men have had our share of botching things up from time to time."

"I like this story, Captain." Otto thought of his own country in Russia and the way his people were treated by Czar Nicholas who ruled his country and nodded his head in agreement. Then he remembered how Catherine the Great had forced all Jews to move to a certain area of land and changed his mind. *There can be unjust cruelty from both sides,* he thought.

"Speaking of learning new things, I *still* have a strong desire to know what the P stands for in your illustrious name."

Mac looked at Otto and laughed. "Well, Otto, I must admit, when you get something in your mind you're like a dog on a bone. If I tell you what the P stands for in my middle name, will you promise not to go blabbing it all over camp?

" I promise on my poor Papa's grave to never tell a soul."

Mac exhaled a deep breath of air. "My parents must have had an unusual sense of humor when I was born. It was bad enough that they named me *Cornelius* as a first name. But to further torment me, they branded me with the middle name of *Percival*. Imagine, Cornelius Percival McAuliffe. If only they had known how I was teased by my school mates. So you must promise me, Otto, that you will take my secret to the grave with you."

"I think I can see why you might not want others to know this name, but I am honored that you shared it with me. I will keep your secret close to my heart."

"Hello Otto!" At that moment, Otto looked up to see Victoria walking toward their camp with a book in her hand. He smiled and waved at her. "Excuse me please. I would like to read with Victoria before it gets too dark. Do you have need of me at the moment, Captain?"

"No, Otto", the captain said with a smile. "Go and practice your reading."

Otto and Victoria made their way to the same spot in which Otto had been sitting before being called to dinner. The pair took off their shoes and dangled them in the chilly shallow shore of the river. The summer evening still held the warmth from the day and the refreshing water tickled their toes.

Mac had told the members that after the summit, the group would follow the trail near the American River which would take them down the western slope of the mountain and into the Sacramento Valley.

Victoria cleared her throat and said, "Pa says we'll be leaving the wagon train in about ten days to head off to my uncle's farm."

Otto felt a tightening in his chest. He glanced at Victoria and wondered how he could bear to say goodbye to his friend. Over the past months, the two had been through so much together. "Where is your uncle's land located?"

"Ma saved every letter her brother wrote over the past five years. I must have read them over a hundred times on this trip. The land is near a place called Fairfield. Uncle Bob and Aunt Imogene bought fifty acres of farmland near a wide delta. My uncle says the land is fertile and the westerly breeze from the Pacific Ocean is perfect for growing all kinds of crops. There's plenty of water for irrigating the fields and the mild winters make it easy to produce food all year long. Aunt Imogene wrote that with all the folks coming into California, they can hardly stay on top of the large demand for wheat, corn, and the other fruits and vegetables they produce on their land. That's why they invited our family to come and settle on their farm. They have cleared a spot for our house and are looking forward to the extra help to cultivate more land for crops."

"It is good to have your family waiting to take you in." Otto thought of his own family scattered every which way and wondered if he would ever see any of them again.

"Otto?"

"Yes, Victoria."

"Pa says you'd be more than welcome if you'd like to come and join us on the farm. He says there'd be plenty of work for you and your wages would be fair...." Victoria's voice trailed off into silence.

Otto was almost moved to tears with the generous offer from the Dickerson family. He surprised himself by reaching out and gathering Victoria's hand into his. He was amazed at how much smaller her hand was compared with his own as he cupped his fingers around her more delicate ones. Otto exhaled a sigh of relief that Victoria seemed content to let him hold her hand in this way. He thought of the friendship the two had formed over the last five months while sharing their love of reading and books. He grimaced at the thought of the twister and the knife that had nearly killed his young friend. Otto turned to face his companion and noticed that her eyes were wet with tears. Their bond was so great, that it was as though she knew the answer to her family's offer before Otto even spoke.

"Do not be sad, my friend. It would be wonderful to be able to go with your family to your uncle's farm. You have all been so kind to me. It was this way from the very start of our journey." Otto thought of his misery at the hands of Bull and added, "I know I would have had a much harder time without the kindness of your family, but I cannot accept the kind offer you have put forward to me. I must go to San Francisco and try and find my brother, Ivan. I have come too far to turn away from my journey."

"I knew it, but Pa wanted me to ask." Victoria reached up with her unfettered hand and wiped away a tear from her cheek. She turned and smiled at Otto and asked, "You'll write to me won't you?"

Otto smiled back at her and said, "I will write to you often and, with the grace of God, I will come and visit you one day on your farm with the wonderful news that I have been able to reunite with all my family in California."

Chapter 20 ~ October, 1854 – San Francisco

The young wrangler gripped the sides of his pony with his thighs. The gesture helped steady the insides of his stomach, which felt much like a tumble weed whirling in a twister. Otto sniffed the air and looked at the scene unfolding before him. The streets of San Francisco bustled with the movements of people dressed in a variety of different outfits from their native countries. Otto inhaled. It seemed the air he breathed crackled with excitement. He could feel the muscles in Hawkeye's neck tense-up as he threaded his horse down the crowded street. "Easy, boy," murmured Otto, I know how you feel." He bent over and stroked the side of the horse's neck and whispered, "I'm a bit nervous myself." The pony relaxed under the gentle hand and soothing words of the rider.

To one side, Captain McAuliffe rode Dickens, and on the other, Kirby sat astride his brown steed, Buck. Otto felt oddly protected by the men flanking his sides against the ruckus unfolding around him. He wished that Biscuit, Gray Owl, and Little Feather had come to town with them, but the three had chosen to camp away from town and stay with the remaining two covered wagons and spare horses.

"What do you think of it all?" Mac asked Otto.

"There's so much sparkle and excitement in San Francisco! Once I get used to all the banging and noise, I think I'm going to like this place, Captain."

McAuliffe laughed.

Otto eyed the new construction going on in the city. The pounding of hammers tapped out a lively rhythm in his ear, and the grating of saws against wooden boards sent the piney smell of sawdust to his nose. Otto breathed deeply and smiled. Despite the many new buildings rising up from the ground, there was a scrappy look to the city. A sturdy new brick bank and a brightly painted hotel appeared out of character next to a makeshift restaurant. The poorly constructed building, framed in wood and covered with canvas siding, looked like a stiff wind might blow it over. A brightly colored sign nailed over the front door said:

Special of the Day:
Bear Meat and Beans
$5.00 (in gold) ~ fer a plate.

An open-air Chinese laundry shop stood next to the tipsy restaurant. Its roof had been covered with colorful strips of thin cloth to shield the workers from the sun. The bright yellow, green, and red strips of cloth fluttered in the breeze like a shimmering rainbow. Inside, a large iron caldron rested atop a wood fire with glowing red coals. Steam rose from the pot and became trapped under the colorful canopy of fabric. Otto saw three men with shiny black hair pulled back and braided in long strands down the back of their necks. Although the men were small in stature, powerful arms and shoulders pulled boiling pieces of cloth from the caldron with long wooden poles and dumped them in a pile on a large table. With deft hands, two women grabbed from the steaming pile of material, extracted a garment, and attached the item to ropes stretched tight across the area for drying. Otto wondered how the women could handle the scalding garment with bare hands, but they did not seemed bothered by the process. One young girl glanced over at him as she pegged red long-johns onto the line. One of the men barked something to her in Chinese, and she quickly went back to the table for another item of clothing.

Otto's eyes opened wide to an array of people clothed in colorful dress from various parts of the world. Captain McAuliffe noticed the curious look on Otto's face and pointed out the different ethnic groups. "Folks from all over the world have converged on California, Otto, hoping to strike it rich. That man by the saloon door, with the large black hat trimmed with silver and fancy riding boots, looks to be from Argentina. Those women hanging clothes on the line come from China, and the two men bartering for fruit look to be from Chile."

Kirby pointed out a beautiful senorita walking along a wooden-plank sidewalk. She moved gracefully in a blue taffeta dress and wore a matching lace scarf attached to her hair with a tall comb. An older Indian woman, who looked to be her servant, walked behind the young woman. Otto watched until they entered the door of a dry goods store.

Otto anxiously scanned the faces of everyone milling about the street. "I wonder if Ivan is here."

McAuliffe pulled a cloth from his pocket and coughed into it. Otto glanced over at his boss, but, gratefully, the coughing fit was quickly over. Mac stuffed the hanky in his jacket pocket.

"You must be excited, Otto, finally to be here."

"I am, Captain."

"Well, let's head up the hill to the *Ruby Slipper Palace* and ask around. If you want to know what's going on in San Francisco, you can bet Ruby May has heard about it."

"Who is this Ruby May?"

"Well, pound for pound, she's just about the smartest business woman I ever met. Ruby owns the *Ruby Slipper Palace* along with a bunch of other real estate in San Francisco. She, also, happens to be a friend of mine."

Otto looked at Captain McAuliffe and noticed his eyes light up as he talked about his friend.

"I shall be happy to meet this lady friend of yours, Captain. And I hope she might have some good news for me."

Otto, Mac, and Kirby got off their horses and let a young groom lead the animals off to a stable for watering and grooming. Otto looked up at the building and shook his head in disbelief. The *Ruby Slipper Palace* was, without a doubt, the grandest building in town. Situated at the top of a hill, it stood alone like a grand castle. Unlike the many other saloons and hotels Otto had seen in town with swinging doors, Ruby's establishment was more like a hotel. The men walked up wide brick steps, lined with flowering bushes in large clay pots, to the front entrance. Otto's eyes were drawn to two elaborately carved wooden doors. Above the doors, hundreds of ruby-colored glass stones had been set in a large wooden sign hanging from an intricate wrought-iron frame. The glass stones, formed in the shape of a glittering red boot, sparkled in the sun. Above the boot were the words, *Ruby Slipper Palace,* which had been painted in fancy black and gold lettering. Otto thought the presentation was clever, without being gaudy.

A doorman tipped his hat and pulled on a fancy brass handle. One of the doors glided open to reveal a lobby fitted with red carpet and beautiful oil paintings in gilded frames. The three men removed their hats in unison and stopped to admire the room.

Captain McAuliffe whistled softly and said, "Ruby May has made some improvements since we were here last year, Kirby." He scratched his head and chuckled. "I always knew she was the best business woman (or man) in San Francisco."

Otto gasped when he looked up to see a high ceiling. The top edge had been painted in a burgundy strip about a foot wide. A pattern of gold twists and swirls were painted over the burgundy base. In the middle of the ceiling, shiny golden stars on a dark blue background twinkled like the night sky. Otto took in a deep breath and let it out slowly. The lobby contained potted palm trees and an assortment of marble statues. These were placed near neatly arranged sofas and chairs where folks could sit and visit in quiet. To the left, a curved polished staircase led to the second floor. Off to the right, Otto saw waiters setting tables with crystal and china in what looked to be a fancy dining room.

Directly across from the main lobby, a well-dressed dark-skinned man pushed open a matching set of double doors and led four gentlemen out of, what looked to be, a large gambling saloon. The doorman was enormous. His skin gleamed the color of smoky copper, and his hair coiled in tight rings around his face. He looked to be about thirty. Despite his easy smile, this broad-shouldered giant commanded respect. Otto knew the doorman was there to do a job and he felt the man would not tolerate any nonsense from the patrons inside the saloon. Music, laughter, and the musty scents of smoke and whiskey floated into the lobby like a cloud until the door closed in silence.

The doorman escorted the men to the center of the lobby. "Thank you, gentlemen, for honoring the Ruby Slipper with your patronage."

A handsome and well-dressed man with green eyes turned and said, "The pleasure was ours, Timothy. Why, that's the most fun I've had since opening our new bank on Union Street. Tell Ruby she's done a fine job with her establishment and we'll call again soon." The banker placed several bills into the doorman's hand.

"Thank you, Mr. Mars, and Ruby sends best wishes to your lovely wife." Timothy nodded and smiled as the men crossed the lobby and headed for the double doors that led outside.

Before they reached the exit, two doorman greeted them with smiles as they thrust open the double doors to the outside.

Otto noticed that a large black carriage had been brought around and awaited their arrival at the bottom of the staircase.

Timothy glanced over in their direction and a wide smile of recognition spread across his face. "Captain McAuliffe. My, my, my, but ain't you a sight for sore eyes. Ruby's been expecting you might be showin' up any day now." Timothy looked at Mac with a furrowed brow. "Is everything okay, Captain? You look a bit like a half-starved coyote."

McAuliffe met the doorman with a firm handshake and said, "Nothing that a bath and a good meal won't fix, Timothy. Could you arrange that for us? We'd like to get the dust off our hides before we present ourselves to Ruby. Seems as though she's been doing quite well this past year."

"Yes, Captain. Miss Ruby is a fine business woman. I'll take care of that for y'all right away." Timothy walked the men over to the registration desk and told the man behind the counter to set the gentlemen up with three of their finest rooms and a bath.

Otto soaked his weary body in a large copper tub filled with hot water and washed his hair with fancy soap. It was the first hot bath he had taken since leaving Doctor Simpson's house last spring, and he marveled how something so simple could make him feel so good. Otto wondered if the doc and his family would recognize him. He knew he had grown like a prairie weed over the summer. Otto thought, *When I left New York, I was just a scrappy uncertain kid. So much has happened since then. I feel like I'm all grown up.*

Otto looked around the small room. He could hear the laughter and splashing of the other men nearby. A small table rested in one corner and he could see the Amethyst Bottle he had placed there amongst soaps, shampoos, and sponges. He stared at the bottle and marveled at the many adventures he had been through since Esther had entrusted it into his care.

A knock on the door startled him from his thoughts and he dropped a bar of soap onto the bottom of the copper tub. Otto drew in a breath and reminded himself, *It's not a pack of Crow Indians hunting you down, Otto. You're safe now!*

"Yes?" Otto croaked.

A small Chinese man with warm slanted brown eyes entered the small bath chamber. He carried several large white towels over one arm and Otto's freshly laundered clothes neatly folded in the other . He smiled at Otto and bowed several times. "My name is Benny Sing. I have been asked to help you get dressed and fitted with new clothes. While you be busy washy washy here, Benny Sing washy your old clothes." Benny laughed at his little joke and Otto couldn't help but laugh with him. When finished here please join me in next room."

"Thank you, Mr. Sing. I'll meet you there in a few minutes."

"You call me by my American name, Benny." My most honorable father who lives on the banks of the Yangtze River in China is Mr. Sing!" Then he laughed again at his clever choice of words.

Otto laughed and said, "Thanks, Benny."

Benny bowed several more times, set the towels and clothes on a stool, and closed the door behind him as he exited to the next room.

A few minutes later, after he had dressed and gathered up his bottle, Otto joined Benny in a small adjacent room with a wash basin, a flat iron to press clothes, a table and large mirror in the corner. Two sides of the room were covered with shelves that held bolts of cloth, scissors and other sewing items.

"Mr. Otto, You look very clean from bath. Come see how well you look in mirror."

Otto smiled at the little Chinese man who busied himself in the room. His movements were sharp and efficient. Benny wore loose black trousers and a matching silk coat with a high collar and small buttons that attached at the front. The outfit reminded Otto of a pair of lounging pajamas he had sometimes seen Doctor Simpson wear in the evenings in New York. Otto thought Benny's clothes looked very comfortable and perfect for the type of work he did.

"Captain McAuliffe ask Benny to make new clothes for Otto. He say ones you are wearing now not fit so good. You stand here, and Benny take many measurements. I make for you chop, chop. Be ready tomorrow."

"What does this mean, chop, chop?" asked Otto,

Benny Sing laughed. "It means very fast!" After the measurements were taken, Benny moved several bolts of fabric to the large table and set about cutting the cloth.

Slowly Otto made his way to the corner where a large mirror was attached to a wooden stand. What he saw took his breath away. His pants were six inches above his ankles, and the shirt on his back was stretched across his wide shoulders. The sleeves met half way between his elbows and wrists. Otto knew that he had grown in the months he had been on the wagon train. He just didn't realize how much. His skin had a warm golden glow from the many weeks spent outdoors. Thanks to the steady supply of good food, from Biscuit, he no longer resembled that skinny kid who lived by his wits on the streets of New York. Otto was shocked at how healthy and strong he looked and felt.

Chapter 21 ~ October 1854 - San Francisco

Otto slept the better part of that day and night. So much worry had been lifted from his mind. He knew that Hawkeye was being well cared for and fed. The bed he slept in was as soft as a cloud, and the sheets smelled of lavender soap, which reminded him of his mother. True to his word, Benny delivered his new clothes to his room that morning. The sturdy denim pants and red flannel shirt fit perfectly. A new cowboy hat and the freshly polished boots, given to him by Levi Wise, completed his outfit. Otto had been asked to meet Mac and Kirby in the dining room for breakfast. He gathered up the Amethyst Bottle and placed it over his shoulder as he walked out of the room.

Otto was directed to the dining room by the large man known as Timothy. He walked toward where the captain and Kirby sat with a beautiful woman, which he assumed to be Ruby May. The woman was laughing at something the captain had said. Mac looked very handsome in a smart pair of black slacks and black shiny boots. A brocade vest covered a crisp white shirt and silk tie. To Otto, he looked very much the handsome aristocrat in these clothes. Otto briefly flashed an image of the Englishman, Sir Nigel Churchstone in his mind. McAuliffe's face was freshly shaven and his hair had been trimmed neatly but not too short. Ruby was looking at him with a warm smile, and Otto could sense how fond they were of each other. Otto thought Mac looked ten years younger than the man that had been his trail boss. He also noticed that the captain was still not smoking.

Ruby had beautiful blue eyes and lovely brown hair which she wore up with soft curls framing the delicate features of her face. She stood up with the men when Otto neared their table. She possessed a small nose and determined chin. Otto noted that she was tall for a woman, but Otto still looked down at her as she greeted him.

"Why Otto, I have heard so much about you from Mac and Kirby that I feel as if I already know you." Ruby grasped his hand in hers and flashed a big smile. Otto saw that she was dressed in a crisp silk dress the color of spring grass that stopped just above her ankles. Her feet were adorned with delicate little red boots with fancy heels. The boots came up to her ankles and were tied with matching silk laces. "I see you're admiring my red shoes. They're my calling card you might say." She pointed Otto to a chair and said, "Let's sit down and get to know each other. The boys have been telling me that you're looking to find your brother, Ivan, and I have some promising information for you."

Otto could hardly contain his excitement. "This is fine news indeed!"

"I have a good friend who works at the bank on Union Street. I thought we could go see him after breakfast. He holds accounts for many of the men who work in town or who work claims in the mountains. He may have information for us."

"Will you be joining us, Captain?"

"Yes, I have some business to conduct there myself. Kirby is going to check on Biscuit, Gray Owl, and Little Feather. I thought we could ride over and join them after we finish at the bank."

Ruby motioned for a waiter to come to the table. "What would you like for breakfast, boys? You must be as hungry as a Grizzly bear!"

Mac and Ruby sat in the large spacious office of Russell William Mars who was better known as RW to most of his friends and clientele. "It's good to see you again Mac. I wondered if that was you in the lobby at Ruby's but wasn't sure. You look more as I remembered you, today."

"Dust and grime can do that to a man!" said, Mac.

"Let me say, Mac, you were wise to invest as a silent partner with Ruby May. As you can see, she has made good use of your money, and today you are a very rich man."

Ruby spoke. "Mac placed his trust in me when so many others would not. He holds a special place in my heart." Ruby May reached over and took Mac's hand in hers.

In truth, Cornelius had little to spend his money on while he led the members across the United States over the years. He had met Ruby seven year's ago when she was running a small establishment in town known as the *Ruby Slipper Saloon*. He wasn't into gambling or fancy living so it was simple to invest his hard-earned money with a woman as smart as Ruby May. Mac could see that she was bright and good with money so it was easy to say yes when she asked him to go in with her as a silent partner to expand her business. The pair trusted each other and over time had formed an alliance that grew into feelings for each other that were much stronger.

"Well now that our business is concluded, let's see if we can help young Otto." RW fetched Otto who was sitting in the lobby of the bank. "It's a pleasure to meet you. The captain thinks very highly of you. Do you wish to open an account? Our interest rates are fair," said RJ as he escorted Otto to his office.

"Yes, I will be putting my money in your bank. I am also looking for my brother whose name is Ivan Stanoff. I was wondering if you knew of him. He may have an account with you."

"Unfortunately, it is against bank policy to share that information with you. Sit tight for a minute and let me check on a few things." RW was gone for about five minutes, but returned with a smile on his face and a young attractive woman in tow. "Although I can't say if he is or is not a client here, one of my file clerks had dinner with a man that might fit the description of your brother. This is Sarah. I think she may know your brother."

The girl looked at Otto and spoke softly. "Mr. Mars says your name is Otto. Is this right?"

"Yes."

I had dinner a while back with a friend that I think might be your brother." Sarah blushed. "We met in the bank and have been seeing each other for this past year. His name is Ivan and he left again for the gold fields several week's ago. He told me about his family in Russia and that he had a brother named Otto. He said his mother wrote to him to be on the look-out for you. Ivan is very much a gentleman and has been saving his money to bring his family to California."

"This is best news! Do you know where he has gone?"

"He has a claim in the mountains outside of Angels Camp near Sonora. He told me he was going to work his claim for another month before coming to stay in town for the winter. He has done well in the gold fields and has made enough money to bring his family out soon." Sarah smiled. "I hope this helps. You look a lot like him."

Otto thanked Sarah. "I hope we meet again soon."

With that, Otto opened an account at the bank and deposited most of his wages earned while working on the wagon train. He felt very grown up.

Mac and Otto met in the lobby of the *Ruby Slipper Palace*. Mac had changed into his riding clothes, He held a flour sack that had been packed with food and other supplies. On the way back from the bank, the group had gone into a mercantile store. Otto had purchased a warm coat and some other equipment for his trip to Angels Camp. With that, the two headed to where Gray Owl and the others were camped outside the city. Otto asked the captain to hold the Amethyst Bottle on the ride out. He had been doing this for several weeks and Mac was fine with obliging him. Mac thought, *It may be a coincidence, but I have been feeling better. And I don't seem to miss the tobacco as much.*

"The weather in this place is very pleasing for October. In Russia and New York, the weather would be much colder."

"That's true, Otto. This land is so much more that gold. The soil is fine for growing all sorts of food. I think when more people hear about this place, it will become a very popular destination. There's talk about running railroad tracks all across the prairie one day. That will make this place explode. You might want to consider buying land."

Otto thought about this and said, "This is a fine idea, Captain. In Russia, not many Jewish people own land. I like America. But I will not buy land near this place that might explode."

Otto was surprised when the captain let out a roar of laughter.

Otto and McAuliffe looked toward the camp where they had, but a few days before, parted ways from Biscuit, Gray Owl, and Little Feather. They saw Kirby chatting with the group while holding a plate of Biscuit's food.

The riders tethered their horse near the other horses to graze on grass. The camp was set up near a small stream.

Little Feather was smiling and talking to Gray Owl in Lakota. Gray Owl explained, "Little Feather is wanting to tell Otto about the many fish she has been catching with her hands."

Biscuit remarked, "They aren't all that big, but they are mighty tasty."

"It is good to practice your special gift," said Otto, once again speaking the beautiful language of the Sioux.

The group settled around the campfire to discuss future plans. Mac explained that he would be retiring from leading emigrants across the country and offered to give all his supplies, including horses and wagons, to Kirby and Biscuit if they wanted to take over the business. The pair jumped at the opportunity.

Biscuit asked , "What about Gray Owl?"

Gray Owl addressed the circle of friends and said he and Little Feather would strike out on their own and would be leaving that life behind. "I have spoken of our plans with the captain. We agree that the way of the Sioux Indians, who have roamed the prairie hunting buffalo, is coming to an end. I have come to see that more and more settlers will swallow our native lands with ranches and farms. I see troubled times for the future of all Indian tribes. The captain has helped me see that it would be wise to buy some land and start a business. Little Feather and I will raise horses and cattle to sell to the many settlers coming here. They will need these animals to start their new life. The captain said he would help me buy the land so there will be no problem for us."

Captain McAuliffe spoke. "I have enjoyed the many years of friendship with you on the trail. In the process, I have become a very rich man with too much money for me to spend." He reached into his vest and handed an envelope to Biscuit, Kirby, and Gray Owl. This is just my way of saying thanks, The only stipulation is that I want you to check in with me at least once a year,"

"Heck, Captain, we would have done that anyway. But this generous gift sure does help a lot," said Kirby. "Biscuit and I will get our supplies and head out in a few days. We want to hightail it over the Sierra's before winter. If the weather holds out we will continue east to Fort Bridger, then on to Elm Grove and the next batch of emigrants hoping to head west. With just the two of us, we will be able to make quick time."

Biscuit looked at Otto and asked, What about you, Otto? Any news on your brother, Ivan?"

"I will ride to a place called Angels Camp where, I think Ivan might be working his claim to find more gold. The captain has made a kind offer to go with me, but I have said no. He has done too much for me already and he will start to retire. I think this is the right word."

Mac nodded and said, "I don't know how much fishing I'll be doing. Ruby has big plans for us. But first, I plan to ask her to marry me." The friends offered congratulations, until Gray Owl put up his hand to speak.

"Otto will not make this trip to gold field alone. No! Otto is brother to Gray Owl. You brought Ghost Walker back to the land of living by finding Little Feather. Slowly, you teach me how to feel whole again with your stories and happy character. We will face this new journey together."

After much talk it was decided that Little Feather would go back with Mac to the Ruby Slipper Palace to stay until Otto and Gray Owl returned from the Sierra Mountains. Mac knew that

Ruby would take the girl under her wing and acquaint her with life in contemporary society. The group spent an enjoyable afternoon together knowing that this would be the last time they would be together for awhile.

Chapter 22 ~ October 1854 - Angels Camp

Angels Camp was just one of the many gold mining camps that dotted the foothills of the Sierra Nevada Mountains known as the Mother Lode Country. Millions of dollars were mined from the area which was set amid towering Redwoods and abundant streams. For thousands of years Native Americans, who roamed the area, held the ancient Giant Sequoias as sacred.

Otto and Gray Owl tethered their horses outside a sturdy log structure run by a shopkeeper named Henry Angel. Henry started the Trading Post at the beginning of the 1848 Gold Rush and had the town officially named after him in 1853. Miners from all over the world inhabited the area. Most prospectors had only one idea – mining gold. When they were in town, they often squandered their gold on whiskey, gambling, and women.

A large contingent of Chinese immigrants occupied the town. When not digging for gold, they made money doing a variety of jobs. Their passion for work and the willingness to do jobs as cooks, laundrymen, and repairmen, made them a valued part of the camp.

"Good day strangers. My name is Henry Angel. What brings you to Angels Camp?"

"Good day to you, sir. My name is Otto and this is my friend, Gray Owl. We are looking for my brother who has a claim for getting gold in this area. His name is Ivan Stanoff."

The storekeeper had seen all kinds of different folks pass through his store, so he wasn't at all curious as to why this foreigner would be traveling with an Indian.

"You say his name is Ivan?"

"Yes, do you know him?"

"Of course. The Russian has been working a claim near here for over a year. He stays pretty much to himself. He rarely comes to town, and I've never seen him squander his gold on gambling or drinking whiskey in the saloon. Rumor has it that he's done pretty darn well in the fields, but like most of the prospectors, Ivan stays tight-lipped about that."

"This is wonderful news. Do you know where we might find him?"

"I know his claim is near an area know as Cripple Creek, but it might be hard to find on your own. You probably should ask one of them Chinamen to take you there. They know every inch of this area and might be willing to help. Mind you, they're good hagglers and will be happy to take advantage of a new greenhorn in town. Try to settle on a few dollars. There's a cook that runs an eating place up the street. His name is Li Wu. He'll hook you up."

Otto thanked Henry Angel, and he and Gray Owl led their horses in the direction of Li Wu's restaurant. They noticed men playing cards. Some were whittling with their knives and one fellow slept peacefully in a hammock strung between two stately pine trees.

"Seems like the gold diggers like to rest when they're in town. Gray Owl, you did not talk to the shopkeeper. Why were you so quiet?"

"Gray Owl find that it's better to listen and not speak much until asked a question. I have learned it is better this way."

Li Wu barked orders at the young Chinese girl that had just finished bringing hot tea to the other Chinese that were working near camp that day. "PJ, fill the large cauldron with water and set the pots near the fire. The men will want their tea again in the afternoon. You such lazy slave girl. I sell you down mountain to be singing girl in brothel if you not work harder!"

The insult was unfair because the young girl worked like a mule fourteen hours each day for this tyrant. Li Wu had bought the girl at an illicit slave-trading operation in San Francisco when she was nine-years-old. Many Chinese coming off the boat did not realize it was illegal to be sold this way. It was so common all over China.

As hard as the work was, PJ was grateful not to have ended up as a singing girl like so many others. She shuddered when she thought of that life. "Yes, honorable sir." She bowed low and carried the heavy pots to the kitchen to make more tea.

PJ performed many tasks like chopping wood for the stove and endless washing for the eating place. She knew the area well. Often Li Wu would send her out delivering mail or notes to the prospectors. She was sometimes rewarded with a few pennies, but the coins were always handed over to the master. She had been warned that to keep them meant a beating from Li Wu. The girl's most taxing job was delivering tea. Three times each day Li Wu had the girl fill two large iron pots with scalding tea which she then attached to a long pole by the heavy iron handles on the pots. A ladle was set inside the pots for distributing tea into enamel cups which the Chinese workers always carried on their belts. Three times a day, the girl was made to squat low as the pole and the pots were lifted onto her shoulders by Li Wu. In the beginning, PJ strained the muscles in her legs to lift herself and her burden to a standing position. When the weight of the heavy load caused an imbalance, she spilt the tea. This angered Li Wu and she was cuffed in the head. But over time, she came to master the task without spilling a drop of the jasmine tea, and the girl grew very strong.

The Chinese men in the camp had an arrangement with Li Wu. They paid him one dollar each month for the privilege of being served the tea three times each day. It was very profitable for Li Wu. No profits went to the slave girl. Her reward was a meager amount of rice with a few slivers of meat that she was given twice a day, and the right to sleep in the corner of the kitchen next to the stove at night to keep the fire from burning out. She dreamed about flying away like a graceful crane, but there was no place to go. Her life was a living hell.

Otto and Gray Owl entered the eatery and asked for the man named Li Wu.

"I am Li Wu. How may I be of service? I could serve you soup from a recipe given to me by my honorable ancestors. It be best in camp!"

Otto introduced himself and Gray Owl to the old man and explained their reason for being there, and how Henry Angel had thought he might be able to guide them to the area known as Cripple Creek.

"I myself am most busy with restaurant, but if we settle on agreeable sum, I have my lazy worker take you there. The three settled on a price that seemed reasonable and Li Wu yelled to the back, which looked to Otto like a small kitchen.

"PJ, you worthless dog, come here. I have job for you!"

Gray Owl and Otto had been on the trail leading to Cripple Creek for twenty minutes. At first, the young girl had gestured that she wanted to walk ahead of them, but Otto said they were in a big hurry and that she should ride on his horse behind him. Reluctantly, she nodded her head. She was used to being told what to do by Li Wu. She knew that any objection would lead to a slap on the head or a kick to her backside. PJ wanted no trouble with the strangers.

At Li Wu's instructions to the girl at the restaurant, PJ had not spoken a word - only nodding her head and bowing, and Otto wondered if she were a mute. At length, Otto said, "My name is Otto and this is my good friend Gray Owl. We have come all the way across the prairie and over two large mountains from the east. I come from Russia and Gray Owl is an honorable member of the Lakota Sioux tribe." Otto was not certain PJ understood what he was saying but he continued. "I heard Li Wu call you PJ. That is an interesting name. What does it mean?"

PJ wondered if she should talk to the men. Li Wu had instructed her *never* to talk to anyone but him. She decided to remain silent.

The day was warm and Otto grew thirsty. He pulled the Amethyst Bottle from its leather pouch and took a long swig of water. Gray Owl followed by drinking from the skin Little Feather had taken from Boiling Pot the night they left the Crows sleeping by the fire. Otto handed the beautiful bottle to PJ and motioned her to drink.

PJ had been working since dawn and she was very thirsty. Grasping the bottle with unsteady hands, the girl gratefully drank some of the refreshing liquid. She looked at the bottle and without thinking, she spoke.

In the most stunning English accent, PJ expressed, "This bottle is most beautiful. The brilliant color reminds me of a field of lavender I once saw when I was journeying to Hong Kong to be sold into a household to work. The morning sun sparkled on the flowers from a recent rain. The color held so much beauty to my eyes that I wanted to stay looking at the wondrous scene before me, until my master pushed me forward and told me to hurry. Such beauty was rarely ever seen by me. The colors of my life have been only gray and black. Funny that I should think of that now."

Gray Owl and Otto were riding side by side, and they looked at each other in utter amazement. Otto immediately thought of Sir Nigel and his butler Simon because this girl spoke with the most beautiful British accent – like an aristocrat.

At length, Otto composed himself and said, "That is a lovely story. The bottle has a way of reminding people of past experiences in their lives. Thank you for sharing it. If I'm not being to rude, I heard Li Wu call you PJ. This is a name that is unusual to me. Might I ask, what does it mean, and where did you learn to speak such beautiful English?"

"The California name that I gave to myself when I arrived here became PJ. The Chinese name given to me by my mother is Yah-Ying. I was born the fifth girl to my parents who were very poor farmers. In China, girls are not held in high esteem. Only sons are revered. So when I was six-years-old, my parents sold me to a man for a small sum of money. From there, my life became very hard."

"This Chinese name, Yah-Ying sounds pleasing to my ear. Why change this name to PJ?" asked Gray Owl.

"By an odd twist of cruelty my Chinese name, Yah-Ying, literally means Precious Jewel. Trust me when I say, I learned early in life that I was nothing like a precious jewel. It would have been better to name me Dung Beetle. On my travels as a slave, I came into the lives of some English missionary people that were living in Hong Kong. My master wanted me to learn the language of the 'foreign devils' who were teaching about this man called Jesus at the school, He said to understand these barbarians, I must learn the language so to know how they think, and to pass this knowledge to him. At first, I was scared that I might fail, and I knew this would anger my master. But the language came easy to me, and I liked that alphabet contained only twenty-six letters compared to the hundreds of Chinese characters."

PJ sighed wistfully and said, "Thus came the English accent taught to me by the British missionaries." PJ looked wistfully at the bottle and sighed. "But that was a lifetime ago."

Gray Owl nodded and said, "I know what it is like to not want to honor the name you were born with. I understand your wish to want another name."

"When I arrived in San Francisco, I found it easier to not speak too much. It seemed better to become invisible to those around me. I had one advantage which was to understand the English words without people knowing I could. It gave me a slight feeling of power. When I was asked what my name was, PJ came forth from my mouth. I took a name, that was less than a name. I knew I could never call myself, Yah-Ying." PJ laughed, "Precious Jewel, indeed."

"You have had a very hard journey. Gray Owl and I know something about hardship and we can relate to what you have been through. With permission, I believe we would find honor if you would let us call you, Yah-Ying."

"I will grant this wish, but you must never let anyone know my secret."

"Yah-Ying, knowing how to speak English gives you many advantages in this country. Besides it is illegal to own a slave in California. This is a free state. You do not have to stay with Li Wu. He does not *own* you!"

"I will give what you say some thought. Could you tell me a little about this beautiful bottle?"

For the remainder of the journey to Cripple Creek, Otto let Yah-Ying hold the bottle as he shared many tales of Tara and Esther and how the bottle mysteriously changed color with each new owner. The girl was found the stories enchanting.

Chapter 23 ~ October 1854 - Cripple Creek

Yah-Ying tapped Otto on the shoulder and said, "Please stop here. The way to your destination is just up this trail. It is easy to find. I must leave you now and make my way back to Li Wu. He will be angry if I am not there to deliver the tea."

"But, it's a long way back," declared Otto.

"It is not hard for me, as I am very strong in my legs and lungs. I will fly down the hill like a crane. Yah-Ying must once again become PJ and take up my miserable life in the camp. But this short time spent with you both will give me many hours to think and day-dream of the bottle, and the stories you shared with me. For that, I am most grateful."

"Remember what Gray Owl and I told you. In California, a person can not own you like a horse. Try to get away." Otto told Yah-Ying about Mac and Ruby. He told her where to find the Ruby Slipper Palace and promised her that his friends would help her. Yah-Ying waved goodbye as she raced toward Angels Camp, and Otto yelled, "I will tell my friends to look out for you."

True to Yah -Ying's word, the trail took Gray Owl and Otto to a small river. They came upon a prospector panning for gold near the edge of the Creek.

The man looked up and immediately pulled his gun from its holster. "State your business strangers!" His eyes were steely gray to match his scruffy beard which was also gray.

"My name is Otto and this is Gray Owl. We wish you no harm. We have just come from San Francisco, and I am looking for my brother, Ivan Stanoff. We were told, in Angels Camp, that he is working a claim along Cripple Creek. Do you know him"?

The prospector lowered his gun but did not put is back in his holster. "Well I'll be darned. My name's Buster. Sure, I know Ivan. He works a claim about two hundred yards up the creek where the water makes a bend in the stream. Wish I had his claim. I think he's got a right sweet little spot. So yer his brother! I think I may see a family resemblance. Sorry to draw my gun on you, but ya can't be too careful around these parts. The Dalby brothers, Jake and Erik, were robbed last week. Said a man wearing a bandana across his face snuck into their camp, as they were eating dinner, and relieved them of about two hundred dollars in gold. When the robber tied them to a tree, they saw a missing finger on his left hand.

"Did you catch him?"

"Nope, but we will. We have what we call prospector's law in the gold fields. If a man is caught stealing another miner's gold, a trial is held and if found guilty his finger is cut off. Let's others know he's a thief. Second time he's caught, he'll get the noose!"

"What is this noose you speak of?"

"It's a rope which will be tied around his neck, and he'll be hung from a tree. Be careful up here." Buster put his gun back in his holster and pointed in the direction they should go.

Otto tipped his hat and waved goodbye to Buster, as they nudged the horses toward Ivan's claim.

Otto and Gray Owl decided to walk their horses into what appeared to be Ivan's camp, so as not to startle him. A small campfire with rocks circling the edges had been formed in a clearing of dirt. An enamel coffee pot rested on an iron grate next to a pot of beans. A canvas tent was set back a few feet from the fire. They could see a man crouched near the water about ten yards away.

Otto called out, "Ivan, is that you? It is your brother, Otto, who has come to find you." Before Otto had barely finished the sentence, Ivan came running up from the creek.

In Russian, Ivan exclaimed, "Otto! Can this be true? Mama wrote to me saying she received a letter from you that you were starting work on a wagon train and might be coming this way, but I thought it was too much to hope for."

The brothers hugged each other and started to cry. After a few minutes, Ivan asked, "Who is your companion?"

Otto composed himself before he spoke. Excuse me, Ivan. Do you speak English? I would like to introduce you to my good friend, Gray Owl."

"Yes, I am slowly learning the language. I have a book and a good friend that helps me. But please, let us sit by the fire." Several logs had been placed near the fire and the three sat down.

With that, Otto started speaking English so that Gray Owl could be included in the conversation. "This is my good friend, Gray Owl."

Otto and Gray Owl spent the next hour telling Ivan about their time on the wagon train sharing the many adventures that he, Mac, and Little Feather had on their journey west.

Ivan scratched his head in amazement. "I must say, Otto, your English is good. You always were a smart kid."

"A very good friend of mine that I met on the trip west taught me. Her name is Victoria."

Ivan teased, "I think this Victoria may be someone you like, yes? And look at you, little brother. You have grown tall like a stalk of corn since I last saw you. You now carry a gun and a knife, just like a man."

"The story of the gun and the knife will be saved for later, but I would like to share something special with you." Otto took the pouch from his shoulder and placed it in his lap. He took the Amethyst Bottle from its case and handed it to Ivan.

"This is most beautiful. The color reminds me of the amethyst stone in the crest Mama always wore around her neck."

Otto smiled and pulled the crest from under his shirt and handed it to Ivan. "Mama was so sad when you were taken from her that I think she could hardly bear the soldiers taking me too, so she entrusted me with the crest until we all could be together as a family again."

"Awe, little brother. Then I have a very good surprise for you. Mama and the little ones have been booked on a ship that will arrive in San Francisco in two weeks. I have pretty much gotten all of the gold out of this claim and was planning on leaving here in a few days. This is almost too much to believe. My heart is filled with such joy." He handed Otto the crest and said, "You should be the one to give it to Mama when we meet her at the dock."

The rest of the afternoon was spent showing Gray Owl and Otto the sluice box that Ivan had built to catch the heavy nuggets of gold that were caught on the wooden rungs at the bottom of the box. Ivan shared that he had done very well in the gold fields and he was ready to start a produce business in San

Francisco and settle down. "Vegetables and fruit are much in demand."

Gray Owl decided that he would take his rifle and bow to look for some small game for their dinner.

"There are lots of rabbit and squirrel in the area. This would be good gift for me. I am often so tired at end of day that some hardtack and stale beans from breakfast are all I can muster up."

With that, Gray Owl slipped quietly out of the camp to hunt for supper. Dusk was approaching and the brothers realized they had been talking for a long time. Ivan said he would go wash up in the creek and gather more wood for the fire. Otto decided to retrieve the bed rolls he and Gray Owl had brought along. He was bending down to stoke the fire when he heard footsteps crackle in the dead pine needles. "Is that you, Ivan." Otto turned around to see his brother with a gun pointed at his head.

"You best not try anything or your friend will have his brains scattered in the dirt."

Otto could not believe his eyes. Staring at him with a snarl on his face was none other than the man who had made his life a living torment on the wagon train. "You!"

Bull snarled, "I thought that might be you, Jew boy. Must admit, you've grown so much I hardly recognized you. This party just gets better and better, and I plan to exact sweet revenge. Now walk slowly on over here and drop your pistol and knife. If I'm not mistaken, I think they belong to me."

Otto could see no way to get the upper hand. Ivan had left his rifle in his tent and was unarmed. He removed his pistol and Bowie knife and handed them over to Bull. In doing so, he observed that the index finger on his left hand was missing.

"Now, you two sit on them logs because yer going to give me all your gold.

Ivan asked Otto, "How do you know this man, brother?"

"He was a member of our wagon train until he almost killed my friend, Victoria. He was supposed to be transferred to Fort Laramie to stand trial for murder."

"That's right, but I got the upper hand on those three Calvary men as they slept. I tied them up and stole their rifles and horses. I met up with some renegade Ute Indians and gave them each a horse in exchange for helping me find the wagon train. We were planning to raid the train but you shot me in the shoulder with my own gun."

"The lightning! So that *was* you!."

"You have been a thorn in my backside, but that all ends tonight." Bull turned to Ivan and ordered, "Now, you give me all your gold, or I will drop your brother with a bullet, and I'll only ask you once."

"Don't do it, Ivan."

"It is only money, little brother. Your life is worth much more." With the gun leveled at Otto's chest, Ivan walked over and pushed aside a large bolder. He dug in the dirt and removed a metal box the size of a loaf of bread, and handed it to Bull.

That's just fine. Bull looked at Otto and said, "Now you can remove that fancy bobble from around your neck. I'll be taking that too."

Otto had completely forgotten that he had not put the crest under his shirt. He was devastated that, after all this time, the crest, that he had so carefully worn next to his heart, would be lost to him. He was sick with grief.

"I'll be relieving you of that pretty little bottle, as well. Remove it from your shoulder and hand it over."

For Otto, it was the final realization that Bull would not only take all their possessions, but would most likely kill them as well.

Slowly, Otto removed the strap from his neck. He started to hand the case to Bull, but in a last desperate moment, his grief turned to rage. Otto swung the bottle toward Bull, just like he had with the mountain lion, and hit him in the face. The action caused Bull to stumble backward and Otto decided to pounce like the lion. Otto had grown a lot in the past months, but Bull outweighed him by at least fifty pounds. Ivan was knocked to the ground as Bull and Otto wrestled in the dirt. Bull used the bulk of his weight to pin Otto to the ground. He lifted the pistol still in his hand and pointed it to Otto's temple. He motioned to Ivan. "Move and I'll shoot you where you lay in the dirt!"

Bull wiped blood from his lip and stood up. "You have been a pain in my butt for some time. I'm going to enjoy putting a bullet in you. But before I watch you die, I will watch you squirm over your precious possession. I had to sit around camp and listen to you tell Kirby and Mac about how you done slain that mountain lion with yer bottle. Well I ain't no lion. With that, Bull picked up the Amethyst Bottle by its strap and hurled it into the creek.

Otto watched in horror as the bottle and case floated down the fast-moving creek and out of sight. His heart felt hollow inside. With that, Bull leveled the pistol that Otto had been carrying these past months and aimed it at Otto.

The shot was so loud it echoed off the rocks and into the twilight.

Stunned that he was not dead, Otto turned and saw smoke coming from the barrel of Gray Owl's rifle. A turkey lay in the dirt next to his feet.. Otto felt numb. Every movement after was like he was in a trance. He could not untangle what had just happened. Ivan and Gray Owl remained planted in their places. They stayed frozen, staring at the man crumpled in the dirt for what seemed like an eternity.

But what was, in actuality, a very short period of time brought several miners running from up and down the creek brandishing rifles and guns. Otto saw Buster among them.

Buster walked over to where Bull lay crumpled in the dirt. He noticed that one finger was missing from his left hand, and he also noted that the man was dead.

It took the better part of an hour to explain what had happened in the camp. At the end of the story, Buster spoke for the other miners. "This looks a lot like the description of the man that robbed the Dalby brothers." One of the other miners had found a satchel nearby with a quantity of gold inside.

"I think we can, without a doubt, call what happened here self-defense. And, in truth, if the scoundrel had only been wounded, he would have hung anyway. That's the prospectors punishment for stealing a miner's gold a second time," said Buster.

The prospectors picked up the thief and carried him off for burying.

Gray Owl fed the campfire with some twigs and logs. The fire did little to warm their mood. "It is never good to take the life of another, but this man was going to kill you, Otto."

"Gray Owl, you did the right thing. Ivan and I would be dead if it was not for you. We are lucky that you came back when you did."

"What do you think made this man, Bull, so angry with life?" asked Ivan.

Otto thought for a moment. "I don't know. Maybe he had a hard life, or a mother who didn't love him, but we've all faced hard times. I guess, rather than rise above those hardships, he became bitter and made himself into a victim."

"I hope he goes to Great Spirits and finds peace. We will never know," added Gray Owl.

The three slept fitfully that night and awoke early the next morning. Gray Owl and Otto searched, in vain, for the Amethyst Bottle, as Ivan packed up his belongings. Ivan had decided it was a good time to break camp. None of them wanted to stay in that place of death. By midmorning they were headed down from the gold fields to San Francisco.

Epilogue ~ October 1855 - San Francisco

Otto smiled as he looked at the scene before him. The reception room of the Ruby Slipper Palace was filled with ferns and flowers. Mac and Ruby had made a lovely couple reciting their marriage vows before the minister only moments before. Otto thought Mac looked rested and content in his fancy suit, as he looked down at Ruby dressed in a long white gown. Shiny red boots poked out from under the hem of her dress as Mac whirled her on the dance floor to a Viennese Waltz.

Otto sighed with happiness. Everyone he loved had made it to the wedding. Biscuit and Kirby sat at one of the tables with Gray Owl and Little Feather. Otto smiled at Little Feather who was just beginning to show that a new life would be coming into their circle in a few months. The horse and cattle ranch that Mac helped them buy was just starting to turn a profit. Otto nodded at his brother, Ivan, who had just asked Sarah to join him on the dance floor. The pair had recently announced their engagement to the family. Sarah's boss, Mr. Mars and his lovely wife stood up to join in the merriment. Otto waved at the doorman Timothy, and Benny Sing standing in a corner with some of the other employees of the hotel. Otto was thrilled that Levi Wise and his family had come. They were doing so well making shoes for the people of San Francisco. Already, Otto had asked the cobbler to make him a new pair of boots. It seemed that his feet just kept growing. Sir Nigel Churchstone and Simon Walton had delayed their voyage back to England just so they could share in the festivities. They told the wedding party that they would be sailing back to London in a fortnight.

Otto glanced at Mama talking to the little ones Sophie, Anna, and Levi. Otto thought Natasha looked beautiful wearing the amethyst crest around her neck. Ivan and Otto were happy to buy her a gold chain for her birthday. Last year, they had arrived just in time to help Ivan and Otto complete the finishing touches on their new store on Market Street. They decided to name their green grocery store, *Stanoff ~ Family Fresh Produce*. The produce they provided had become an instant hit with the growing population of San Francisco. When Otto wasn't working in the market, he drove their new wagon to buy produce at wholesale prices. He soon found that he had a talent for acquiring contracts with several farms in the area for various fresh fruits and vegetables. The family became the main vendor to Ruby and Mac for their popular restaurant at the Ruby Slipper Palace. Otto's favorite time was visiting the Dickerson's farm to load up on supplies. It gave him a chance to catch up with Victoria and share the new books they were reading with each other.

Otto looked across the dance floor and watched as the Dickerson family burst out laughing at something Chandler had just said. At that moment, Victoria looked across the room at Otto and smiled. She stood up and made her way over to where Otto stood near the edge of the dance floor. Otto watched his friend and thought she looked beautiful in her new gown, as she gracefully moved toward him. The beautiful violet-colored satin ribbon adorned her hair. They smiled at each other. Their joy was evident in their eyes. "You look pretty tonight, Victoria." And the violet satin ribbon complements your blue eyes with lavender around the edges. Shall we dance?" Victoria nodded and smiled. Otto extended his hand and together they joined the others on the dance floor.

Yah-Ying had been plotting her escape from Angels Camp for a year. She had managed to save some of the money given to her running errands by only giving half to Li Wu. She took on extra jobs washing and mending clothes for the miners. When Li Wu demanded her earnings, she stood up to him and told him that the money she earned on her own belonged to her. To her amazement, he only grunted at her before walking away. As the months went by, Yah-Ying grew stronger. Slowly she was finding her voice.

Summer passed and Yah-Ying knew winter was just around the corner. On one quiet autumn night, she left the kitchen fire stoked with wood before quietly making her way to where she had hidden a few supplies for her journey away from the gold fields. She walked all night to get as far away from Li Wu and her miserable life as possible.

Dawn was breaking in the east and Yah-Ying was tired and thirsty. She left the trail and walked over to a stream to wash her face and drink from the enamel cup she had tethered to her belt. Yah-Ying gathered strength from the cold liquid. She sat at the edge of the water and thought, with excitement, of the journey that lay before her. Lost in her thoughts, the girl barely noticed a muddy leather case caught up on thorn bush growing near the creek. She stared at the object for some time. Something about the case looked vaguely familiar. She waded into the shallow water and released the case from its imprisonment. She decided to clean the sandy mud from the leather pouch before opening it to see what was inside. Slowly, Yah-Ying reached her hand inside the case and pulled the Amethyst Bottle into the light of the morning. She gasped at the sight of the bottle. *This is Otto's bottle. I wonder how he lost it? I will go to the place he told me about and return it to him.*

At that moment, the bottle began to change. Yah-Ying suddenly remembered Otto telling her about the mysterious bottle and how it would change colors when it went to be with a new person. The girl was awe-struck as she witnessed streaks of red, gold, and black burst across the surface, much like the fireworks she had once seen in Hong Kong during Chinese New Year. She sat on the edge of the stream mesmerized by the sudden changes coming over the bottle. After some time had passed, the bottle had lost all traces of the beautiful shades of lavender and purple that had adorned the Amethyst Bottle.

Instantly, Yah-Ying understood that the bottle had now come into her possession for a reason. She knew that it had been placed in her care to help her find her way on her own journey. Yah-Ying looked at the beautiful bottle and instantly a thought came into her head. The words that came forth were so vivid. It was as though her honorable ancestors were speaking to her from afar. She cradled the bottle in her hands and pronounced out loud, "I will call you the **Mandarin Bottle**."

* * * * * *